"We're here."

Clare's eyes shot open. "Where?"

"My mother's."

"Your mother's?" She swallowed hard. What on earth was he bringing her here for? She was meant to be another one-night stand, not taken home to mother! She looked down at her breasts, struggling to escape her skimpy red dress, the indecent amount of leg she was showing and her striking red stilettos…with the discomfort, she guessed, of a lap dancer at the opera. *What had she got herself into?*

Mark took Clare's hand as he helped her out of the limousine. He tried not to smile. He'd certainly surprised her—she looked positively put out. "Problem?"

She flashed him a smile. "No, of course not." She smoothed out her dress, looking for all the world as if she was searching for extra length. "Flattered, really."

Darcy Maguire is the newest Australian author
to join Harlequin Romance®.

You'll love her fresh, contemporary style,
brimming with emotional warmth!

Men who turn your whole world upside down!

Strong and silent…
Powerful and passionate…
Tough and tender…

Who can resist the rugged loners of the Outback?
As tough and untamed as the land they rule,
they burn as hot as the Australian sun
once they meet the women they've been waiting for.

ACCIDENTAL BRIDE

Darcy Maguire

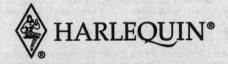

TORONTO • NEW YORK • LONDON
AMSTERDAM • PARIS • SYDNEY • HAMBURG
STOCKHOLM • ATHENS • TOKYO • MILAN • MADRID
PRAGUE • WARSAW • BUDAPEST • AUCKLAND

ISBN 0-373-03754-6

ACCIDENTAL BRIDE

First North American Publication 2003.

Visit us at www.eHarlequin.com

Printed in U.S.A.

CHAPTER ONE

SHE was to die for.

Mark King couldn't help but look at her. He darted glances from the dance-floor, noting the other men in the room, young and old alike, drawn to her like yuppies to Wall Street. They had no idea.

Mark, however, knew she was dangerous. His heart pounded in his chest and his blood fired to the challenge. And she'd be a challenge—he raked her boldly with his eyes—every sexy inch of her.

She stood as tall as the group of men who swarmed around her, dwarfing them in both stature and style. The light fell softly on her from the chandeliers of the hotel ballroom, setting off burgundy highlights in her dark hair—hair that was swept back to her nape, small wisps escaping to frame her ivory face.

Pearl drops hung from her ears and a string of pearls fell low over the swell of her breasts. Mark closed his eyes and could almost imagine trailing his lips over her skin.

He led his date closer to the stranger, moving slowly with the music, his eyes drawn to the long black gown that hugged the woman's shape faithfully, and to the curves that made his hands itch with the need to touch. The split in her dress ran almost the entire length of her long legs—legs that captivated him with fantasies of what they'd feel like wrapped around him.

Mark saw a bearded man close to her, intimately close, possessively close, almost touching his suit against her bare shoulders. His gut clenched tight. He dropped his gaze to her hands—not one ring on *any* of her fingers—and let out a breath he hadn't realised he'd been holding. *Who was she?*

'Mark!' Sasha's voice scraped on his fantasies. 'If you don't want to dance, just tell me. These are new shoes.'

Mark looked down, dimly aware of his size ten and a halves on the tips of Sasha's shiny red shoes. 'Sorry.' He moved back onto the floor, noticing the score had changed, as had the rhythm of the music. He willed himself to focus on something other than the sexy stranger.

There was always more than enough work to fill his mind. Tracking down the next challenge, the delving and the searching for weaknesses in a company, the thrill involved in acquiring it, and the dissecting and selling off to make every dollar spent multiply for him.

What sort of job would Miss Femme Fatale have? A model? A designer? Or maybe she survived as a professional heartbreaker, progressing from one relationship to the next, consuming both bank balance and heart? A fleeting urge to find a place for her in his company surged from his loins—he could see her occasionally, often, always...

'Excuse me,' said a silky voice. A perfectly manicured, unvarnished fingernail tapped Sasha's shoulder.

Mark looked directly into deep blue eyes that were unafraid to gaze right back at him. His breath caught in his throat. The sexual magnetism that made the stranger so confident radiated from her. Drew him in. Stoked a growing fire deep inside him.

Mark couldn't tear his eyes away. Her ivory face had a soft flush, as though an artist had carved her delicate features from marble then dabbed her cheeks with colour. Her dusky-rose lips were full and tempting, and her royal blue eyes danced over him in a way that sent bolts of desire coursing through his body. A small scar interrupted one finely arched eyebrow, suggesting she was indeed human after all and not some exquisite work of art.

Sasha dropped Mark's hand and swung around, her face set grimly to confront the interloper. 'Yes?'

'I'm cutting in.' The stranger's voice rang with command as she unhesitatingly took Mark's hand and stepped into his arms. 'You don't mind, do you?'

Mark tried to hide his amazement.

He didn't hesitate.

He slid his hand around her waist and the heat of her body ignited his blood and mind to fantasy again. He encased her slender fingers in his and swept her across the dance floor.

A tremor of excitement ripped through him at her light touch on his shoulder. Her appeal was devastating, and her creamy skin felt as smooth and silky under his hands as it looked.

The sensations that radiated from her warm hand to his took him by surprise, while his other hand at the small of her back threatened to fall lower.

Mark took a deep breath, filling his lungs with the sweetly intoxicating scent of roses that surrounded his stranger.

He couldn't pick out what it was about her that made his body react to her. He'd seen many beautiful women before, and even had a few throw themselves at him. But this woman, she was different, and the need to find out exactly how pounded deep in his chest. 'To what do I owe the pleasure?'

Clare had been irked Mark King hadn't noticed her grand entrance, but the thrill of knowing he'd been watching her was enough to give her the extra bit of courage she needed to take the plunge and cut in. Now she had him where she wanted him.

'I was bored.' She raised one shoulder in the slightest hint of a shrug. The swell of satisfaction was bolstering. King was lured by the bait; all she had to do was get him to take the hook and reel him in. Guys were so easy to interest.

'Bored?' The comment seemed to surprise him.

'Oh, yes,' she breathed softly, glancing around at

her audience. Clare hadn't expected her outfit to attract quite so much attention, but it served the purpose, and maybe the attention everyone else was giving her would motivate King and his over-sized ego right into her ambush.

After what Mark King had done, she was going to stuff and mount him, nailed directly through the heart. He wouldn't know what had hit him.

King would look sensational mounted on her apartment wall, she thought crazily. His jet-black hair and olive skin would go well with her decor. His strong jawline, handsome square face, and the generous mouth that promised to be as seductive as the rest of him, would be far more interesting to look at as she sipped her morning tea than her print of Cézanne's *Still Life*.

'Why would a woman as beautiful as you be bored?'

The rich timbre of his voice tingled down her spine. She shrugged, allowing a smile to touch her lips. 'Don't you ever feel that there aren't any challenges left in life?'

King's gunmetal-grey eyes glinted mischievously. 'I know exactly what you mean.' He pulled her closer to him, her soft curves moulding to the contours of his hard body.

They fitted so well together, she thought traitorously, then rejected the notion. She wasn't going to think of the *enemy* that way—and he was the enemy. What he'd done was unforgivable. She'd had it with

men and their games. This was the last straw in a
series of griefs and it was well past time she evened
the score.

He expertly swept her around in a circle, as if he
were as much at home on the dance floor as in the
boardroom. She supposed he thought he was God's
gift to women. He held her firmly, the warmth of
his embrace so male, so bracing, so damned annoying.

Clare hadn't expected him to be quite like this.
She'd expected someone colder—not this hot-
blooded specimen that called to her primal urges. It
was no wonder that women succumbed so easily to
his charm.

She could feel the hard muscle of his shoulders
under his black suit, feel the power in his body, feel
the promise throbbing from him that he'd be an experience to remember.

Clare wasn't about to lose her head, though. She'd
had enough knocks in life to know the truth about
men and relationships—*all* liars and *all* lies. No
matter what he could make her body feel, what
magic he might weave, she was impervious.

The anguish her last boyfriend, Josh, had left her
with had cured her of any romantic notions. She bit
her lip at the unwelcome surge of pain that accompanied her memories. It amazed her how she had
been drawn into believing in love—the quiet dinners, the beach walks, the moving in. And then *bam!*
It was over. And she hadn't had an inkling that

something was wrong until she'd found Josh packing.

How could she have been so blind? He'd been slipping away from her the moment he moved in: right into someone else's loving arms. And she'd been too busy to notice.

She could have done something, she figured. Changed somehow. *If* she'd realised. He was married now, to that woman. Her neck muscles tightened—she'd never feel his cheating lips again.

She'd been a gullible fool. But not this time. Clare was prepared. Forewarned. Steeled for this. And she was glad she could look Mr Tall, Dark and Dangerous straight in the eye, thanks to her generous heels.

The music stopped and they stepped apart, applauding the orchestra with the rest of the crowd. She had to concede that the Excelsior's grand ballroom made the perfect location for King's charity dinner. The polished timber floors, the extravagant chandeliers of imported crystal and the twenty-piece orchestra all furthered his cause—to romance the money from his guests' pockets.

Clare leant towards King and brushed her lips against his warm cheek. 'Are you game for one?' she whispered.

His eyes glittered dangerously. 'One what?'

'A challenge,' Clare said casually. And she turned on her heel and walked away from him, vividly aware of his gaze following her. She forced herself to breathe through the onslaught of butterflies in her stomach. Step one was over; the plan was in motion. She just had to reel him in—and nothing was going to get the best of her, especially Mark King.

CHAPTER TWO

MARK scanned the room, his eyes searching the crowd for one extremely intriguing lady. He knew he shouldn't have taken his eyes off her, but locating Sasha in the crowd next to the dance floor had been all it took to lose sight of her. Brunettes were everywhere, but none with the height, the split in the dress or those haunting deep blue eyes.

'Who the hell was that woman?' Sasha snapped, hooking her arm in his possessively.

'I have no idea.' But he was determined to find out. If she was as fascinating and mysterious as she'd intimated, he wanted to discover every detail about her—down to what underwear she wore. Or didn't.

'And you let her embarrass me like that in front of all these people?' Sasha swung her arms wide, her cheeks flushed.

Mark forced himself to focus on his date. His blood cooled at the hurt in her eyes. The deal was to introduce Sasha to the notables of society, and he'd all but ignored her. 'I'm sorry. I didn't think.'

'Well, I'd appreciate it if you did think. I don't know how I can look anyone in the face now.'

Agreeing to a date with his sister's best friend

wasn't the cleverest situation he'd got himself into, but he had needed a companion and Sasha had been available and there were no strings attached. And strings were what he wanted to avoid.

Mark caught a glimpse of his stranger. She certainly was a vision. She was so confident and so perfect that he knew there had to be a catch.

He had no idea what she meant. Was she challenging him? And, if so, to what? His mind buzzed with the possibilities—and they all ended with his stranger naked and in his bed.

Mark shook himself. This was crazy. The last thing he'd expected at this charity night was a woman like her. He was here to raise money for the Heart Foundation, to give back to society, to give his life some meaning beyond the size of his bank balance.

His own heart thrummed a call he couldn't ignore. There was no reason he couldn't pursue the woman *and* serve the charity…

Mark strode to the entrance of the dining room and hailed the head waiter. He leaned close to the man's ear. 'Seating has been changed. See that woman.' He cast a look to his stranger, who was in a conversation with a gangly man. 'I want her at *my* table.'

'Certainly, sir.'

Mark smiled, straightening to his full height. He walked through the doorway, smiling to his guests. If she thought he was going to play along with her game she had a surprise coming. *He* was going to get some answers.

Clare wasn't surprised when the waiter extricated her from the man she was talking to and escorted her to Mark King's table. She would have been disappointed if he'd done anything less. From what she knew about him he was finding life a tad boring now he'd made it, and was taking on all sorts of challenges for the thrill alone. She figured his personal life wouldn't be any different.

Clare had noted that he managed to keep his exploits out of the papers—and his photo. Which was probably why she was so surprised by King in the flesh.

Clare glanced around the dining room. It was laid out with over fifty round tables, all with white tablecloths overlaying burgundy ones. She couldn't miss the lavish bouquet of roses that adorned each table, or the careful positioning of the cutlery, glasses and elaborately folded serviettes. Of course King wouldn't settle for anything less than stylishly elegant.

She lifted her chin. The perfect venue for her trap. Public enough to be safe; private enough to get away with what she was about to do.

Everyone else was seated when Clare arrived at the main table. She cast a lazy glance around the guests, taking in the heavy-set men accompanied by wives laden with expensive jewellery, the younger men with pretty companions hanging on their every word. And Mark King.

'Welcome, Miss...?' King rose from the table and gestured to the chair on his left. On the other side was the woman in red she'd ousted on the dance floor.

'Thank you.' She ignored the question and allowed him to help her into her seat, aware that all eyes were on her. He moved her chair in and she felt his knuckles brush the skin on her back, causing an irritating shiver to course down her spine.

'I'm afraid I'm at a loss.' King's voice was deep and demanding, his gaze sharp.

'I find that hard to believe.' She took a sip of champagne, casting him a look of defiance from beneath lowered lashes. She'd been in business long enough to hold her own in company such as this.

King took his own seat, leaning close to her. 'Are you avoiding giving me your name, or are you just playing coy?' he whispered with a vague hint of annoyance.

'I assure you, I'm not playing.' Clare could hear the edge in her voice and added a smile to tone down her slip.

She saw King raise an eyebrow. 'What's your business, then?'

'Much the same as yours, I'd say.'

King turned in his seat to give her his full attention. 'Why did you walk away like that?'

'Like what?' she asked innocently, very aware

that most of the occupants at the table were hanging on their every word. It surprised her that he'd confront her so openly, in front of his guests, but then King was about the most arrogant, self-assured jerk she'd ever met. He probably didn't care what anyone thought of him.

A muscle in King's jaw twitched. 'I personally invited everyone here tonight.' King glanced around the room. 'And I can tell you, *you* weren't one of them.'

'Really?' Clare opened her serviette with a deft flick of the wrist and laid it across her lap. 'Are you sure?'

Clare struggled not to smile. She had him there. She knew he was so busy that he needed three secretaries to keep up with his workload, plus two personal assistants, both men, which confirmed the fact that he was still serious about work—no distractions. Even his female secretaries were over forty and married, to ensure everyone's mind stayed on their work.

A thoughtful smile curved King's mouth, softening his features. 'You have me there.' He twisted in his seat and raised his hand. 'John?' A man at the next table turned nervously. He rose and approached, his tall, dark and lanky frame looking pretty spiffy in his dinner suit—but then most men looked great in black.

'Yes, sir?'

'John, here, is my personal assistant. He took care

of the invitations.' King smiled. 'John, did you invite this young lady?'

John looked from his boss to Clare, obviously confused. 'Over two hundred invitations went out, sir. But I'll do my best. Your name?'

Clare smiled at King.

'She won't give her name, John. Surely you can remember inviting a young woman?'

John shrugged, looking quite helpless. 'Security is tight, so she must have had an invitation.' John gave Clare an odd look of confusion. 'We could have her taken out, if you wish, sir.'

'Perhaps that would be best.' King's expression darkened. 'If you don't tell me your name then I'll have Security escort you out.'

Clare shrugged. 'If you'd rather throw me out than—' She broke off deliberately, taking another sip of the champagne, casting a look around the table at the curious faces.

'Than what?' His mood veered sharply to anger.

'Than work it out for yourself, then of course— go ahead.'

King stiffened as though she'd struck him. Silence descended on what little conversation there had been at the table. Slowly his tight expression relaxed into a smile that lit his eyes and dimpled his cheek.

Clare felt an unwelcome surge of excitement at the warmth of his smile. She wrenched her attention off King to the roses on the table, taking a long, deep breath. But she couldn't help herself. Her gaze wandered to him again.

King dismissed John with a wave and turned his attention back to her. His grey eyes stabbed her, as though he was trying to penetrate her defences with his look alone.

She slowed her breathing and willed her heart to do the same, praying someone would distract King from her before she lost her nerve.

A waiter laden with a tray of steaming soup bowls moved between them. He placed a bowl in front of her.

Clare looked up at him. 'What sort of soup is it?' The opportunity for a break from King's intensity was welcome. It might even break his train of thought, if she was lucky—if she was *very* lucky.

'It's champagne and pear.' The waiter gave her a smile and a conspiratorial wink. 'All vegetarian, miss.'

'You're a vegetarian?' King pounced. 'That's very trendy of you.'

'I'm not a vegetarian to pander to any social trend.' Clare snatched up her spoon and plunged it into the misty green liquid. She'd be damned if she was going to explain her lifestyle decisions to King! She concentrated on eating, on how the smooth and gentle soup caressed her tastebuds with flavour before slipping down her throat.

'For health, then?' suggested the woman in red next to him.

'Yes.' Clare smiled warmly past King to the pretty young blonde. She'd been so intent on King she hadn't given her a second thought. Shoving her aside on the dance floor was one thing—that was business—but to ignore her over a meal was another. Besides, she had to be barely twenty—just a girl.

'How did *he* know that you were concerned about it being vegetarian?' King gave her another raking gaze. 'Unless they knew you were coming? You phoned them or spoke to them?'

'Yes.' Clare took another mouthful of the divine soup. It was her cousin Paul's creation. She'd had it several times before, while he was learning to be a chef, but this was her first opportunity to dine where he worked without him. Paul was like a brother to her, only two years older than her twenty-seven years, and they were close. They'd grown up under the same roof.

'Yes to which one?' King brandished his soup spoon at her as though it were a weapon.

'Whatever.' Clare shrugged. Paul had smuggled her into the charity dinner, and all she'd had to do was promise she'd accompany him to the next social event to enhance his image. Some career strategy, she guessed.

She broke her bread roll apart and buttered it lazily, very aware of King's eyes on her. 'How do you know Mark?' she asked the girl in red, whose face kept appearing over King's shoulder.

'I'm a *close* friend of the family,' she bit out defensively. 'I'm Sasha Taylor-Jones.'

'Beautiful name.' Clare tried to swallow the smile that was threatening to erupt. The look on King's face at being ignored was priceless. 'You're very kind, doing Mark the favour of accompanying him. He would have been embarrassed to have arrived solo.'

Sasha blushed. 'Actually, he's doing me a favour—though you wouldn't think it.' She cast his back a dirty look and ran a hand over his shoulder. 'Did you know he's just been nominated for Most Eligible Bachelor of the Year?'

'Has he?' Clare smiled her amusement. If only the organisers knew what he got up to with poor innocent young girls, they'd crown him the most opportunistic bastard of the year. She gave Sasha a second look. Was she the next victim?

King's eyes darkened. 'Will you ladies stop talking about me as though I wasn't here?' He swung back to Sasha.

'Mark, don't be angry with her,' Clare chastised him.

'And don't call me Mark. Hell, I don't even know you.'

She could tell it was killing him. If he knew her name then he'd find out everything he needed to know in about two minutes flat, and that wasn't what she had in mind. She had something more memorable planned.

Something that King wouldn't ever forget.

CHAPTER THREE

How her little sister had ended up in King's bed concerned Clare. It wasn't as though they frequented the same circles. King's realm was a world unto itself. Even with her own lucrative transport company's success, she couldn't hope to come anywhere close to it.

The sort of wealth and position he'd built for himself were what dreams were made of. Clare let her gaze wander over his dark hair, his strong jawline, and the quirk of his lips. Surprisingly, he looked quite normal for a millionaire, apart from being aggravatingly handsome.

Meeting King made her goal of owning her entire company seem not so far-fetched. If this guy could do it she was certain she could, too. One day.

'You may not know me. But I do know you.' Clare laid her spoon in her empty bowl and met King's stormy eyes. 'I know your parents split up when you were ten and you spent the next eight years moving from one to the other while your mother searched for love. Your father was declared bankrupt in seventy-nine and eighty-six—when you were ten and seventeen respectively.'

Mark's eyes flickered, and a shadow flashed across his features.

She suppressed a smile of satisfaction—the investigator had been worth the money. 'You studied business economics overseas, then returned to invest your inheritance from your grandparents. Do I need to go on?'

'So you've done your homework.' His voice hardened. 'Are you going to tell me what you're after?'

'No. But I'll tell you this—' She leant close to him, breathing in his spicy cologne. 'We have mutual acquaintances.'

His eyes widened at her admission. 'Ha, it was one of the guys, wasn't it?' He laughed, darting looks around the table. 'Which one of you jokers is responsible?'

Two of the men cleared their throats, three others shrugged, and they all cast curious looks at King.

King snapped his attention back to her, his eyes smouldering.

Clare tried to smother a laugh at his confusion. She had him going. This was even better than she'd planned.

The waiters removed the empty bowls and King dodged around them to see her. 'How long are you going to play this game?'

Clare waited until the table had been cleared, then she leant close to him again. 'Are you bored with me already?'

'Yes.'

But the fire in his eyes told her otherwise. 'Oh, my.' She patted his hand lightly. 'You have it worse than I thought.'

'What?' King's eyes were glued to where her hand covered his.

'Boredom,' she said knowingly, lifting her hand and placing it on her lap, still tingling from the contact. 'You know you age prematurely if you're bored? It can lead to depression and all sorts of mental conditions.'

'Is that true?'

She allowed herself a smile. 'No idea, but it sounded good.' It was like dangling candy in front of a child. Too easy.

A waiter presented Clare with her entrée: a miniature risotto. It was shaped in an oval and topped with caramelised onions. She cast a casual glance around the table—the others had each received a mushroom and ham torte, garnished with snow pea shoots and long curls of carrot.

The touch of King's hand on her thigh almost made her jump. Almost. She hadn't expected it. For some silly reason she'd assumed she wouldn't have to endure physical contact with him until later— much later. There was no doubt now that he was a fast mover.

His fingers stroked her skin, arousing every nerve in her leg, in her stomach, in her entire body. His hand was so warm, so firm and so maddening! He had probably swept her little sister away with his charms before she'd had a chance to think.

'I hope you're not bluffing, Miss...?' His thumb massaged her muscle, working higher up her leg. 'What the hell am I meant to call you?'

'What do you want to call me?' she said calmly. Clare steeled herself against the disturbing sensations his hand on her thigh caused through her body. She took a small bite of the rich rice dish, another of Paul's, focusing on the meal rather than her body's traitorous response to King.

'How about Scarlet?' Sasha offered. 'From that old classic movie.'

'But you're in red, not me.' Clare couldn't help but notice the way Sasha touched King, lightly but possessively. Poor Sasha was laying herself open to King, as good as screaming *Ready, willing and waiting*. If she had any idea where his other hand was...

'You're right.' Sasha chewed her bottom lip, running a hand absently up King's arm, over his nicely built muscles and resting it on his shoulder.

'How about the Black Widow?' King's hand reached the top of her split and traced the edge of the fabric with his fingertip.

Tingles of awareness shot to her toes. 'I'm in black, but I'm no widow.' Clare took another portion of the risotto and put it in her mouth as casually as she could manage, willing herself to chew and swallow without choking, without balking.

The need to slap his hand away was swamping

her. How dared he treat her like this? With no re-
spect for Sasha, no consideration for all the hearts
he'd left behind him, cracked and bleeding.

Clare swallowed the lump of risotto, helping it
down with several gulps of her wine. She looked
dubiously at the small serving on her plate. She'd
hoped to avoid as much conversation as manners
allowed, but she figured having her mouth full
wouldn't last long as an excuse.

'Never been married?' King nodded and scooped
his entrée into his mouth, looking as if he wanted
to get the distraction out of the way as quickly as
possible.

Clare took more of the deep red wine. How was
she going to last an entire evening with King and
his tenacity? She put more risotto in her mouth, then
shook her head, cursing herself for not pacing her
risotto to the questions she didn't want to answer.

The smile on King's face suggested he was
pleased.

'What about something from Shakespeare?' Sasha
glared at Clare as though she was loath to continue
a conversation that didn't revolve around herself, but
beamed at King like a puppy wanting a reward.

'Hmm, Lady Macbeth comes to mind.' King's
voice was deep and husky, his hand caressing her
bare skin with slow, sensual movements designed to
muddle minds. 'We'll call you m'lady, then.'

Clare smiled, covering her disgust. It was all she
could do to let him keep touching her leg without

breaking his nose. After what he'd pulled on her sister... She gritted her teeth, swallowing the tirade of abuse that threatened to erupt.

After her dad had left Clare had looked after her little sister, Fiona, while their mother had worked three jobs. Even living with her mother's widowed sister and her son hadn't eased her mother's burden. The debt her father had left behind had been painfully large.

Clare had pulled strings to get Fiona a job in her office when she'd left school early, unable to cope with the pressure. And she'd retired her mum as soon as her business had made enough to buy a home for her in the Dandenong Ranges. She should have sent Fiona up there too—protected her from the harsh realities of life and men like King.

'Your meal, miss, with compliments from the chef.' A waiter winked at her, then laid a plate in front of her. The rich aroma of the dish drifted upward. It was another of Paul's—a vegetable lasagne with chilli, vegetables and tomato, topped with exotic cheeses.

She concentrated on eating, even though her stomach felt leaden with King's eyes continually on her.

Clare was thankful he needed both hands to tackle his steak. His hand on her leg had been sending a steady stream of interference to her brain. And she needed all her wits about her if she was going to take this guy down.

King ate almost silently, only occasionally joining in the table's conversation and twice responding to Sasha's questions. On the whole, Clare supposed, he was mulling over the facts and trying to figure her out.

'I know you're around twenty-seven, twenty-eight,' King stated coolly, pausing as dessert was served. 'You're in a high position in business, or you own your own. You're well-off, you don't live far away, and you haven't had any serious relationships.'

Clare's spoon stopped halfway to her pastry. She turned to him, her blood pounding in her ears. 'How?'

King's smile lit his entire face. 'Your manner denotes leadership and the quality of your dress screams money. You came in a taxi because of those heels—you wouldn't have been able to drive in them. And there isn't a hint of an indentation or change in colour on any of your fingers, which means you haven't worn a ring in a very long time. You don't wear nail polish,' he continued, sure of himself, 'no fancy rings, only simple jewellery—I'd guess you're a very capable, self-assured woman, not needing all those artificial adornments to enhance the package.'

Clare noticed Sasha pull her hands off the table and tuck them on her lap—her pink-painted nails a dead give-away of her supposed insecurities, if King was to be believed. Personally, she figured he was full of himself—a load of hot air polluting the planet.

King was certainly clever. She had to give him that. But there was no reason she had to pander to him. She stared at the sweet on her plate and took a corner and put it in her mouth. The sheets of buttered wafer-thin pastry were layered with nuts and soaked in a lemony orange-blossom-flavoured sugar and honey syrup. It was heavenly, but it didn't help her brain come up with some clever retort. 'I could have changed into my heels after I'd driven here…?'

Mark knew he was right. He had to be or she wouldn't be looking so demure, being so quiet and intent on her dessert. And he was sure her cheeks had paled a fraction. It was the thrill of the hunt. She was right. He enjoyed a challenge and she was just the sort of challenge he wanted to indulge in at the moment. 'So, do you need a ride home?'

'Are you offering?' his stranger asked, her voice lilting melodiously. She dabbed her full lips with her serviette, staring him directly in the eyes as though daring him to wipe the smile off her lips with his own.

The music resumed in the ballroom and people started drifting away from the tables. Mark, however, had no intention of going anywhere until he had some answers.

He noticed Sasha rising next to him. 'I'm just going to powder my nose.'

Now was the time to interrogate this lady, to give

him a fair chance at this challenge of hers. He could throw all decorum and manners to the wind and seriously terrorise her into the truth without concerning himself with the effect on young Sasha.

Clare rose.

He started. 'Are you joining her?'

'Yes.' She offered him one of her dazzling smiles. 'Will you miss me?'

He rolled his eyes. 'I'll be here.' Working out what the hell she was up to. She certainly was astute—she knew she'd be vulnerable on her own.

The thought that she was some gold-digger had occurred to him. She knew enough about him to know exactly the sort of woman he'd be attracted to. But, hell. Whatever she wanted, however much she cost, the way things were going he'd be up for it—for a chance at taming her.

Mark couldn't help but watch her. She didn't look back. Sasha did, though, and Mark couldn't decide whether his sister's friend liked the woman or was going to have a go at chopping her off at the knees. Mark suspected that Sasha figured he was her territory, but she'd have no joy with his stranger. This was a woman who knew her mind.

Mark had to admit he felt more alive than he'd been for a long time. He liked this game. But he wasn't going to stick to the rules. He hadn't got to where he had by falling in with other people's games. He moved his leg and slipped out her mobile phone from underneath.

Distracting her had been a delight. That split in that dress of hers was perfect. She'd been so soft, so smooth—her handbag and its contents had become almost inconsequential to her leg.

Mark rose and strode to a quiet alcove off the dining room. He turned the small red mobile in his hand. He hoped she'd used it for a personal call and not some weather report that would get him nowhere. But then, there was always the kitchen staff. He didn't have a qualm in the world about striding in there and interrogating them as to how they'd known his mystery guest's dietary requirements.

He flipped it open and pushed redial. A taxi company would be ideal to track down who'd driven her here and from where, but too easy. Mark smiled. The thrill of the hunt pounded through his veins in tune with the peal of the phone.

'Hello?' It was a shaky voice. A woman's. 'Is that you, Clare?'

He rolled the name around his mind. 'Excelsior Hotel. Lost and Found. We've just had this phone handed in and we pride ourselves on service. We'd love to return it to the owner before they leave tonight. Would you be able to describe the owner? I've just pushed redial so you've spoken to them recently. The phone is small and red. Looks like a woman's.'

'It'll be Clare's.' The woman cleared her throat. 'Clare Harrison. She's tall, has shoulder-length brown hair and blue eyes.'

Bingo! A swell of satisfaction rose in his chest. 'Thank you. I'll page her right away.' He rang off, smiling. Clare Harrison. He had her now.

'Isn't that a woman's mobile?'

Mark turned. John was so young and so naïve about the business world and all its shades of grey that became a way of life. 'Yes—yes, it is.'

'You look pleased, sir.'

'Very pleased.' Mark pressed the phone into John's hand. 'Hand this in to a waiter. Say you found it.'

'Yes, sir.' John looked dubiously at the phone and then at Mark.

'Do we know a Clare Harrison? The name sounds familiar.' And he was going to get a whole lot more familiar with the devilish woman.

'Yes, sir.'

Mark snapped his head up. They did? How could they? He would never have forgotten *her*! 'Well, who is she?'

John shuffled his feet. 'She's one of the owners of Trans-International. One of the smaller companies in the pipeline.' John pulled at his tie. 'Why?'

Mark tensed. Trans-Inter. Small and innocuous. Rising fast. A gem to add to his holdings. 'I thought no one knew about our intentions for Trans-Inter?'

'Nobody should, sir. Only a select group involved in researching and compiling the report. You've an appointment to see the other partner on Monday. He owns the majority of the company.'

'I have, have I?' Mark glared at John. 'Under what name did you make our appointment?' Mistakes weren't to be tolerated. John was new, but Mark had made it very clear what he expected of him. If a sniff of his plans were known before he'd got his foot in the door with a partner he'd not only be fighting off the competition but the employees and the other partner...

'Under Mark Johns, sir.'

Mark rubbed his jaw. A clever ruse, and not entirely untrue. John *would* be with him.

So, with that avenue ruled out, how had Miss Harrison found out? And what did she have planned for him? His mind went into overdrive. What would *he* do to save his business if the tables were turned? Anything! He couldn't help feeling that whatever she had planned for him, he was up for it.

Clare Harrison was quite a woman. He would volley anything she could toss his way. And he was sure he'd enjoy the game.

CHAPTER FOUR

FOR a second Clare thought she'd recognised a face as she moved through the crowd, but when she looked again it was gone.

She touched her chest, feeling if her heart was still beating. The last thing she needed was someone who knew her tipping King off and wrecking the plan.

It wouldn't take him long to realise the connection between Clare and her sister and be on to her. Fiona had rung his office number over ten times one day to try and speak with him. Not one call had been returned.

Clare followed Sasha, weaving through the tables and the other guests. The young woman was swinging her hips just a little too much to be believed normal—unless the girl had some spinal problem. It was obvious she was advertising—to Clare as much as anyone—staking her territory.

Clare had met many men like King. They were a dime a dozen. Users, every one of them. Clare felt her blood heat. She'd learnt quickly how to pick them and avoid them. If only she'd helped her sister hone her radar for that type of man she wouldn't be in this mess now.

Clare refreshed her lipstick in the powder room, noticing Sasha watching her intently with narrowed eyes. She could tell what was coming.

Clare replaced her lipstick in her purse and glanced at the young girl who was trying to stare her into oblivion. 'You like him, don't you?'

'Yes. And I want you to know that my father is very rich—and obviously I'm younger, *and* blonde.' She looked Clare up and down dubiously. 'You're wasting your time.'

'I think you'd better take another long hard look at the guy—he's not as innocent as you think. He needs a challenge.' She caught herself before she said too much. 'And he likes *brunettes*.'

Sasha opened her mouth, and closed it.

'He's a man of the world, Sasha. Bored out of his brain with everything. He wants someone who can stand up to him and that's not you. Do yourself a favour and get a nice young man who'll worship the ground you walk on.'

Sasha cocked her head. 'Young guys will worship me?'

'Oh, yes.' Clare sighed. 'Find a nice one and I bet you he won't be turning his back on you for anyone.'

Sasha turned to the mirror and retouched her make-up to perfection. 'You're not just saying that so you get Mark?'

'Take it how you will.' Clare pushed her way

through the large swinging doors and moved back into the ballroom.

She breathed deeply, collecting her thoughts. This was it. Time to lure King back to her place.

The table was empty. Clare swung around. He wasn't hard to find. His jet-black hair, formidable height and expensive suit were a combination easy to spot.

Clare strode forcefully into the alcove, right up to King without hesitation. He smiled when he saw her, a grin that lit his eyes with a dark passion that she knew her sister had experienced first-hand.

Clare didn't falter. She stared at his sensuous mouth and reduced the distance between them. It was time to get serious. Conversation was unnecessary. There was one thing King wanted, and she was all for offering it. Anything to see the guy slighted.

'So, how did you—?'

She covered his mouth hungrily, ravishing it cruelly, trying to smother him as much as she wanted to smother the onslaught of arousal coursing through her.

It took him only a moment to recover from the surprise. His lips danced to life beneath hers, and they were more persuasive and gentle than she cared to admit.

The strong hardness of his mouth tasted so good. Shivers of desire sang through her—an aching need she had denied for too long. A primitive, savage intensity took control and she plundered his mouth mercilessly.

He pulled her hard against him, his hands moving sensuously along her spine, slowing her onslaught with drugging kisses.

King explored her mouth with a gentle mastery, as though tuning her body to his. Every nerve in her body was aware of him, of his warm arms wrapped around her, of the pressure of his body against hers.

A cough next to them intruded on Clare's consciousness. Reality slowly dawned. Where she was, *who* she was kissing and what she was *meant* to be doing.

For a first kiss it had been passionate, hungry, even angry. But it would be unforgettable. Clare pulled away reluctantly. It was far nicer kissing the guy than thinking about him and what he'd done. It wasn't any wonder Fiona had fallen for him. He was a master.

Her lips tingled. Clare couldn't help herself. She tasted his lips again, brushing them softly with hers. She might never feel them again.

'Thank you, John.' King stared into her eyes, his own blazing. 'I think I'll manage from here.'

Clare wanted to slap herself. She hadn't even seen King's assistant standing next to him—she'd been so intent on King that nothing else had registered. Heat annoyingly flooded her cheeks.

She touched her tingling lips, not breaking eye contact with King, using the moment to the fullest.

'Would you like to take me home?' She knew full well what his answer would be. His whole body was primed for *yes*.

'I'd be honoured.' King offered her his arm and moved out through the front doors of the foyer and onto the main road. Clare slipped her arm into his, her body screaming for more of him, her mind alive at the ease with which he was falling in with her plan.

The cool night air gave Clare a jolt back to reality. She couldn't believe she was doing this. She crossed her fingers behind her back, watching the cars speed past. She'd need luck to pull this off.

'On second thoughts, I'll get you a taxi.' King extricated her arm and waved for a taxi. 'It'll be safer.'

Her ego dropped to her toes. 'For you or for me?' she managed. What was happening? What had happened? He was meant to be coming home to her place to face the music.

She stared at her black stilettos and her mind darted over the possibilities, trying to find some way to salvage the situation. But her mind remained blank, frozen in amazed panic.

A smile tugged at his mouth. 'Problem?'

'No, not at all.' She had to play it calm. If it wasn't tonight it would be tomorrow night, or the next. It had to be. Her sister needed it to be. King was obviously hooked. One look at the guy and how he was reacting to her was enough to let her breathe easy. Any moment and he'd ask for her phone number...

A yellow taxi pulled up in front of them and King opened the door for her with a flourish.

Clare stared at him. Her pulse thudded against her eardrums. Any second now he'd ask, or kiss her, or proposition her...

She slid onto the seat. 'Are you sure? I make a mean coffee,' she suggested, while her belly fought the meal. This couldn't be happening. She couldn't make her offer more obvious...

King closed the door of the taxi and smiled. 'Thanks, but no thanks.' He stepped back and gave her a short wave, and even had the nerve to smile at her, his grey eyes taunting her with an unfathomable look.

She lifted her hand and waved vaguely. What had she done wrong? She racked her brain for a hint of what might have tripped her up, warned him off and compromised her ploy. Nothing. She managed a smile for him, praying he was just teasing her, playing with her like a cat played with a mouse. Only she was no mouse.

King's eyes wandered to the traffic on the busy street. He turned and sauntered back into the hotel.

Clare slumped into the seat. All that for nothing! He hadn't even waited to overhear where she lived when she'd given the driver the address.

She swallowed the unpalatable truth. She'd failed. All the planning had meant nothing.

Clare watched the buildings blur as the taxi picked up speed. It was going to take more than a sexy dress to hook King. It was going to take all her brains, her body, and all the bravado she could muster. She just hoped it would be enough.

Clare let herself into her apartment and dropped the keys into a glass bowl on the hall table. Her shoulders fell in defeat. What had gone wrong? She'd been sure she had him hooked.

Clare moved into the kitchen and turned the light on, illuminating her Tasmanian oak kitchen. She never tired of the way the polished timbers looked, how her stainless steel oven gleamed, how it was all hers.

She ran a hand over the smooth surface and moved along the bench. She flicked the switch on the kettle and reached across to a row of jars against the tiled wall. She placed the lid of one of the jars quietly down and dived in. She pulled a chocolate chip cookie out and bit down on the sweet biscuit.

She was at a loss. She didn't know what to do. Clare put the rest of the biscuit in her mouth and took another two from the jar. He wouldn't be calling her. That was for sure. He didn't even know her name.

She kicked off her heels and slumped over the bench.

'Clare?'

The soft whisper of her little sister's hopeful voice

shook her from her mood. She straightened, looking across the open-plan lounge to her sister's room.

'How did it go?' Fiona stood in the doorway, her hands wrapped around herself and her brow furrowed.

'As you can see, honey, not so good.' Clare waved a hand around the empty room, resting her eyes on Fiona.

There was no mistaking that they were sisters. They had the same hair, and the same shape face, but Clare had blue eyes, like her father's, while Fiona had hazel ones. If King had realised who she was and made the connection…

Fiona had tied her hair back, her make-up was subtle, and her fawn linen trouser-suit would have been more at home at the office than in the apartment. Clare cringed. She was dressed and prepped to take Mark on. *If he'd come home with her.*

Although Clare's home had the same rigid tidiness of her office, she allowed lavish colour. This year, her theme was Mexicana. She had cactus and desert grasses in glazed terracotta pots scattered over the polished timber floors, a vibrant crimson and yellow rug lying under her sand-coloured lounge suite, and a large Sombrero hanging from the blue-mottled walls.

'He…he didn't like you?' There was a mixture of hope and fear in Fiona's tone. She moved into the lounge room slowly. 'Maybe he does care. Maybe he isn't as bad as we thought he was. Maybe he just doesn't know where to find me.'

Clare put what was left of her biscuit in her mouth and moved around the island bench. She opened her arms, wrapping her sister in comfort. She swallowed. 'He didn't return any of your calls. And he knows where you work, honey.'

She felt her sister's body shake—and it hit her, sharply in the chest, just how much she hadn't wanted to let her sister down. She'd take on a dozen jerks like King if it meant making Fiona happy.

Clare had spent more time looking after Fiona than her mother had. Mum had always been at work, and apart from Paul's teasing all they'd had was each other. Aunty Rose, Paul's mum, had been too upset with the loss of her husband to notice the living.

Clare held her sister tighter. She had to have done something to tip him off. But no matter how much she racked her brain she couldn't fathom what it was that had warned him off. If she knew, she might have a chance to remedy the disaster tonight had become. As it was…she was helpless.

'Look, you don't need him. You can move on without him.' She squeezed her sister, lightening her voice, hoping her optimism would be catching. 'You have to do what's best for you.'

'Mum figured that, too.' Fiona broke out of her embrace and faced Clare, hands folded tightly across her chest. 'She did what was best for her. And look where that got her. And us.'

'Here, honey. It got us here. We wouldn't be who we are today if Dad hadn't left like that.' Clare touched her right eyebrow, tracing the line of her scar.

'And where is that, exactly?' Fiona bit out. 'Sure, you have money, a place of your own, your independence—but there's more to life than that, Clare. A lot more. And I want that. I want someone to share my life with.'

'Fiona...'

'No, I'm sick of you telling me what I should do. I know what I need to do. And I need him.' She sagged into a chair and covered her face with her hands. 'Maybe you're right.' She lifted her face. 'Maybe I can't have him. But I need to talk to him. Please. You have to do something.'

Clare wrenched the hairpins out of her hair, turning to a small occasional table she'd arranged with colourful maracas and string dolls. 'It'll be okay. I almost had him.'

'Are you going to try again?'

'Sure, honey.' Clare ran her fingers through her shoulder-length hair. Though how she could make it work she had no idea. Tonight should have worked. It should all have been over and done with by now.

'And what happens if he won't come?'

'I guess we'll work it out—*if* that happens.'

* * *

Mark shook the hand of the last guest. It had been a memorable night. One of the best charity dinners he'd ever hosted. The donations had been varied, but on the whole he counted it as a success. Somewhere, some time, some poor soul would benefit from tonight, and a swell of satisfaction filled his chest.

He could have done better, and usually he'd be berating himself for lost opportunities or missed chances. But tonight it was Clare Harrison who still buzzed in his veins. She'd been a great time.

She was right. He was bored. And he was all for meeting her challenge and finding out everything about her.

It was late and he was slowing down, but the memory of her was as vivid and immediate for him as it had been when she'd been in his arms, at his table, taunting his mind. He rubbed his jaw. It annoyed him that he still couldn't work out what her game was. Pre-empting people was what he did well, what he was good at, but he was at a loss here. What the hell was she up to?

'Mark, I'm exhausted. Take me home.' Sasha rubbed a hand up his arm and over his shoulder.

He offered her a soft smile. She'd been extremely tolerant of his behaviour. After Clare had left he had finally given her the introductions she'd come for. Better late than never, he'd figured—though Sasha hadn't seemed as interested as he'd expected her to be after all the fuss she'd made about it.

'Get them to call the car around. I'll be out in a minute.' Mark watched Sasha saunter out of the ballroom, swinging her hips. She was a cute kid, and a great friend to his sister. Jess needed good friends. She'd been through enough and didn't need any more upsets in her life.

Clare had got her facts spot-on. Their parents' divorce had been a traumatic time. Add to that their father losing everything he'd had left to bankruptcy, and Jess barely escaping a wild plunge into drink and drugs, there wasn't any wonder that poor Jess clung to him now for her stability.

Mark figured it was ironic that he now had the lifestyle his father had worked so hard towards. He'd even given his father a loan just last year for yet another venture.

His mother hadn't been there for Jess either. She'd been too strung out trying to find another 'love of her life' to dote on Jess. It had been hard for his little sister to understand. One minute she'd be the apple of her mother's eye, getting shown off to some new man in her life, then she'd be shunted off while her mother went looking again.

His father worked like a man possessed on his get-rich-quick schemes. He'd built his fortune back again in the eighties—until the crash of eighty-six. Then he'd started again. He liked to be busy. That often meant not having time for Jess either. She'd certainly got the short end of the deal as far as parents were concerned, but at least she had him. He'd never let her down. He ran a hand through his hair. He knew first-hand what she'd gone through and what she missed.

He walked out onto the dance floor and closed his eyes, straining to imagine himself in Clare's position. Why would she be issuing him challenges? A ripple of warmth coursed through him. Was she measuring him up as her next business partner?

He sobered. There wouldn't be much of a partnership once he owned the company. From experience, the partners in a newly acquired business never stuck around to see him divvy up and sell it off. They'd take their compensatory cheque and leave him to it, missing the thrill of how much he made of it all.

She couldn't have any qualms about him in that regard. Her research would have given her all the information she needed to know—that he took business very seriously, and that he'd make the most out of Trans-Inter.

Maybe she was seeing how compatible they were? His loins ached. There was little doubt there either. That kiss! He'd never been kissed with such force, passion or intensity.

'The car's here.' Sasha's voice echoed around him.

'On my way.' Mark strode quickly from the room.

The long black limousine sat at the kerb, his chauffeur holding open the door. Sasha climbed in first. 'You're not thinking about that woman, are you?'

Mark cast a glance at her concerned face and bit down on his response. 'Just business. Why?' He slid onto the seat next to her.

Sasha examined her pink nails. 'Because I don't like her. She's not up to *our* class…' She darted him a disdainful glance. 'And she all but warned me off you.'

He relaxed back onto the plush seats. 'Did she?' He couldn't help but feel a warm tingle suffuse his body. 'And what did you say?'

'What did you want me to say?' she asked coyly, moving closer to him. She touched his jacket sleeve and held his arm. She fixed him with a soft look before lowering her lashes.

He was flattered. 'Probably that you're just a friend—so she's welcome to me.' And he'd be so welcoming to Clare. His mind wandered over her body again in his memory. Very welcome.

Sasha dropped her hand and straightened. 'Is that all I am to you? A friend?'

Mark turned to Sasha. 'You're my sister's best friend. That means the world to me.' He saw her eyes glitter. 'But you're far too young for an old bloke like me.'

'But you're only thirty-three.' She wrung her hands together on her lap. 'Is it that you're into brunettes?'

'Pardon?' Mark was caught off-guard. 'Why do you say that?'

'*She* did.' Sasha stared out of the window. 'That woman who cut in. The one you spent all dinner chatting to. The one who has obviously caught your interest.'

'Did she?' So she hadn't just delved into his business life but into his personal one, too. Intriguing. She'd put a lot of effort into finding out about him down to the smallest detail, it seemed.

'I think you owe it to your sister.'

Mark was jerked back to reality. 'To what?'

'To give us a chance.'

'Oh, Sasha.' He framed her face with his hands and kissed her forehead. 'You wouldn't be happy with me.'

The car pulled to the kerb in front of Sasha's family home in the upper Toorak area, where stately homes sat on manicured lawns and European cars adorned the streets.

'Try me,' she whispered softly, her eyes ominously bright. She pulled out of his grasp and opened the door, then stepped out and hurried up the front path. She didn't look back.

Mark rubbed his neck muscles. It seemed he couldn't go out with any woman without getting tangled in strings. He'd have to give up on dates for a while…right after he tamed Clare Harrison.

CHAPTER FIVE

CLARE lay on her duvet, papers spread out around her, wishing her mind would stop torturing her with Saturday night's events. Two nights of restless sleep didn't make Clare a happy girl.

She punched the pillow next to her on the right. It needed it. She hadn't had a man in her bed in nearly two years and it was looking as flat and dejected as she felt.

She hadn't thought of Josh lately. Understandable when she had Fiona's predicament and King to handle. And Mark King was difficult *not* to think about.

Clare focused on the papers at hand, trying for the life of her to hang onto the grand visions she had for Trans-Inter. She would make it great—if she could keep her mind on the job at hand and not King's irritatingly handsome face.

She'd seen enough of life to be tough. She'd chosen to follow some opportunities as they'd come her way and had left others. King she'd rather leave, but for now she was stuck with him and the mess he'd created.

It had been a traumatic decision to quit school when she turned sixteen. But she hadn't been able to watch her mother's health deteriorate any further.

She'd worked herself ill with three jobs, and it had been obvious to even a young Clare that her mum wasn't able to keep going.

Frank Bolton, the owner of Trans-Inter, had taken her on as a junior office gofer, teaching her the ropes and challenging her mind with tasks that had required her to think. She'd become his personal assistant at the company in a matter of years, even though it had only been a twelve-truck-two-office-staff operation. It had been a dream come true to support her family. And Frank had encouraged her to study at night school and acquire skills to help improve the company.

He had been her boss for a good five years before his wife had tired of him. Facing losing his business in the divorce settlement, Frank had been prime for Clare's offer. She'd bought his wife's share of the business for a more than reasonable sum.

Clare closed her eyes. The inheritance from her mother's father had come at the perfect time for her. If only the old man hadn't been so stubbornly attached to his farm and his principles her mother's life wouldn't have been so hard, or lonely. And he might have gone to his grave with family at his side. As it was…

Clare had known the business wasn't at all healthy, despite Frank's claims, but she had eagerly stepped in. And she'd built it up, taking on bigger companies and stealing choice contracts from under their nose.

Streamlining had been the key, and as long as they didn't get complacent now, with their size and contacts, they wouldn't lose money as the other large companies were. Now Frank had all but semi-retired, content to pick up the dividends while she ran the company.

She sighed and lay back on the pillows. Had King known who Fiona was when he'd swept her off her feet? What trouble he was getting himself into? She smiled. She'd certainly make sure he knew it.

Clare tried to read one more document, but the words blurred as Saturday night intruded on her mind again. She touched her lips with her fingertips. If nothing else he was a good kisser.

She jerked and rolled off her bed, gathering up the papers and filing them away into her briefcase. There was no way she was going to dwell on him. He wasn't worth the time. She headed for the shower.

Clare wasn't about to let King wriggle free this time, even if she had to handcuff him and drag him to her place. Her mind wandered off on a disturbing tangent and her body sent its approval jolting through her veins.

Clare straightened the cerulean-blue cushions in the lounge room and stood back and took in the picture. Perfect. Just like in a magazine.

She already had a Tahitian fishing theme chosen for next year, and had started collecting knick-knacks and furniture. It was an expensive hobby, but once she'd auctioned off the old theme as one complete set she was often out only a few hundred dollars. Clare wouldn't swap the thrill of finding elusive pieces for anything, and it didn't affect her work at all—she had an entire year to find everything she needed.

She passed Fiona's room and paused. The muffled sound of despair was just audible. She opened the door. Red swollen eyes met hers.

Clare's stomach clenched tight. 'Don't worry. We'll nail him today.'

Fiona wiped her eyes. 'I hope so.'

Clare closed the door, her heart thudding against her ribs. 'Me too,' she murmured.

Clare glanced at her watch. It was almost ten o'clock. She couldn't remember ever being this late for work before—her office staff were probably calling hospitals by now.

She strode through the hallway, glancing into the warehouse through the glass windows that lined the corridor. A glow of satisfaction warmed her at the sight of the bustle, the trucks and the staff. No matter what was going on in her personal life, she could always rely on work to be there for her to throw herself into.

Clare straightened, casting off the tension of this morning's ordeal. Normally she loved the city life. The energy charged her; the ordered frenzy called to her. But this morning some idiot had blocked her car in.

'Good morning, Miss Harrison,' Tanya chimed. Their receptionist was young, bright and enthusiastic.

'Morning. Any calls?'

Tanya handed Clare a wad of messages and her mobile phone. 'You left it at the Excelsior Hotel on Saturday night.'

Clare turned her phone over in her hand. Her purse mustn't have been closed properly...

'You missed the most gorgeous hunk of a man. Mr Bolton said I shouldn't tell you about him, but, goodness, he was...' she rolled her eyes '...*really* cute!'

'Mr Bolton?' Clare stared across the hall to Frank's office. He hardly ever came in these days. He'd bought a boat and spent most of his time fishing and going to clubs. 'Does this man have a name?'

'A Mr Mark Johns.'

The name meant nothing to her. Clare fanned her face with the messages, nibbling on the inside of her cheek. The man might have been a boat salesman, a sales rep or someone unimportant. But why not tell her about him? 'Where was he from?'

'No idea. I don't know what it was about, but he had another good-looking chap with him. They both wore suits. Very professional.'

Clare's muscles tightened. What wouldn't Frank

want her to know about? Although they'd worked together for years, and Clare was running his company for him, Frank had the annoying habit of treating her like someone removed from his own concerns.

She knocked once, then strode into Frank's office. She planted her hands on her hips and glared at her mentor.

Frank met her eyes and his round face flushed—from his bulbous nose to his thick neck, wedged into a white shirt and blue tie. A suit jacket lay over the back of his high-backed leather chair. His eyes met hers. 'Typical. I should have known that woman wouldn't be able to hold her tongue.'

'What's going on, Frank?' Clare swallowed hard. The answer was written as plainly on his face as it was in the quarterly reports—someone wanted the company.

Frank lowered his eyes and concentrated on putting his glasses away. He glanced up. 'Nothing. I don't know what you mean.'

'Don't you?' She prowled around his desk, trying to make direct eye contact. 'We hardly ever see you round here these days—least of all in the morning *and* with a mysterious appointment. And—' she pointed at his attire '—in a suit. Your best one, by the looks.' She paused, letting her accusation sink in. 'Who were they?'

Frank fiddled with a pencil on his desk. 'Clare, you have to understand my position.'

'And what position is that?'

'It's an offer I'd be a fool to refuse.'

'What offer?' Her stomach dropped. She hated being right. 'You could have warned me.'

Frank looked away.

Clare took a step backwards. A chill coursed through her veins. But she'd known it had to come. Had known from the moment they'd landed the biggest trucking contract in the state that their company would catch the interest of some predator. 'Don't tell me you've signed anything?'

She stared at his glasses case. He couldn't have been reading fine print *on a contract*—not without telling her, without talking to her, without caring how much she'd done for him and for the company.

'There's no way you can match it, Clare. I was going to tell you about it. But I didn't want you to get upset.' He shuffled. 'Knowing you'd drive yourself crazy over it, I didn't want you to stress—'

'Hell, Frank. You know what this company means to me.' She clenched her fists. The company was her life. It was her anchor and security for all of them. There was no way she'd ever let her sister and mother go through poverty again. Once was hard enough and long enough to hurt for a lifetime. 'You could give me a chance. I've put everything into this place and I won't have someone coming in and taking over.'

'I'm grateful for what you've done for the old company, Clare, but—'

'No buts, Frank. You give me a week to raise the capital before you sign your share of the company away.'

There was going to be a load of boardroom politics and legal manoeuvring, a zillion meetings to negotiate and navigate around... Unless she got the money together first.

She swung towards the door, angry at herself for not preparing for this, angry at Frank for assuming she hadn't.

'Clare?'

She turned slowly, biting down the harsh retorts on her tongue.

Frank stared at her, his brow furrowed.

She could see it on his face. That she hadn't a chance in Hades. He was probably right. But she'd be damned if she'd give in without a fight. 'Frank, you owe me that.'

Frank sighed. 'Okay, I'll give you forty-eight hours. There's no way I'd want to stall them any longer than that.'

'Who wants it?' Clare bit out. It was an odd thrill that someone had noticed Trans-Inter and wanted it.

'Rulex Holdings.'

Clare flung the door wide on the way out and felt some satisfaction in the crash it made connecting with the thin wall. The name meant nothing to her. Probably a subsidiary of a subsidiary. 'Tanya. In my office. Now.'

*   *   *

The clock in the office chimed twelve o'clock. Clare's coffee had grown cold beside her, forgotten, her focus entirely on convincing someone to lend her the money. She slammed the phone down again, her throat aching at the irony. If she hadn't built the company up so much she'd be able to afford Frank's bloody share. She slashed another bank off her list.

She leant her head into her hands.

She was going to lose control of the company.

Her chest ached. She'd worked her butt off to buy her mother that house, to have a place of her own. Tears stung her eyes. She'd worked so hard for their security, and if she was to have a chance at saving her company she would have to mortgage the lot, putting it all on shaky ground.

The buzzer chimed. 'Clare? Fiona's on line two.'

'Thanks.' She stabbed the button and lifted the phone. 'What is it, honey?'

'I feel weird, taking time off like this.'

'I know. But I think a couple of days to sort yourself out is just what the doctor ordered. Tanya is doing fine.'

'I just rang to ask if it's on for tonight. I'll need to be ready.'

Clare stared blankly at the pencil in her hand. 'For what?'

There was a deep silence. 'If you're bringing Mark King home tonight?'

She sagged. How could she have forgotten that

man? 'Sure, honey. I'm on my way to his office now.'

'You're the greatest, you know.' She rang off.

Clare shook her head. Fiona had no idea! She stood up and smoothed down her trousers, then hesitated. She should never have eaten all those biscuits. She was meant to be attracting the guy! She touched her chin and prayed fate hadn't cursed her with pimples, too.

She gulped down a cup of water and perused herself in the mirror. She sighed. No pimples... But she almost wished there were—she could have used it as an excuse, maybe. She couldn't believe she was doing this now, in the midst of this takeover. The last thing she needed right now was to lock horns with King again—she needed to stay and save her company. But this was more important.

Knowing of her father's and grandfather's indifference to their kin, and how much her mother had suffered as a result, was enough to convince her that, of everything, family held the highest priority.

Clare rallied Tanya with instructions as she strode through the office. The girl could chase down finance for her while she was away. After all, King wouldn't take long to deal with—if he agreed to see her at all.

King's office was as audacious as she'd expected. The building was enormous, with entire walls of glass on every side reflecting the surrounding buildings. She entered the formidable marble-tiled foyer, keeping her eyes ahead, refusing to look up and accept how far out of her league she was.

King was certainly working on grand proportions. The foyer was immense, littered with giant pots of tropical rainforest and scattered with curvaceous abstract marble sculptures. Two security guards stood rigid, like suits of armour, against the walls to either side of the bank of elevators.

The woman at the front desk looked up from her computer and pasted a friendly smile on her face. 'May I help you?'

'Yes, I'd like to see Mr King, please.'

The woman perused her, her eyes narrowing.

Clare threw her shoulders back, confident she'd measure up to the woman's scrutiny. Her grey trousers and white blouse screamed business, although she should have brought her briefcase or at least a manila folder to tuck under her arm.

'Have you got an appointment?'

'No.' Clare shifted her weight. She'd expected this. But it was far more obvious now she was here, and surrounded by all this, that she'd been too hasty in rushing in here assuming she'd get in some way or another.

'Then I'm afraid—'

'I'd like you to let him know I'm here. I'm sure he'll see me.' Clare crossed her fingers behind her back and glanced casually around the foyer.

The woman looked dubiously at her. 'Your name?'

Clare hesitated, but she had no choice. 'Lady Macbeth.' She cringed. She should have pushed for an alternative the other night. Something more normal! But then, this had definitely *not* been the plan.

The woman managed a nervous smile. 'I think you'd better go now, dear.' She beckoned one of the security guards with a flick of her wrist.

Clare tensed. 'I am not *your dear*, and I'd suggest, if you want to still have your job in an hour, you'd better call up Mark. This is no joke.' She held her breath.

Clare could feel all two hundred and fifty pounds of the security guard behind her, waiting for her to make the wrong move, or for the word from the perplexed woman behind the counter.

'What is this in regard to?' The woman stood up. She was obviously floundering in the situation.

'His personal affairs.' Clare began to tap her nails against the counter. 'I don't have time for this.' She took a deep breath. The woman was obviously out of her depth, confused, concerned, indecisive. 'Look, just make the call. If I'm a crackpot, the most you've lost is a few minutes of your time. If I'm not and you don't call…it'll be your job, I assure you.'

The woman lifted the phone hesitantly, her brow furrowed.

Clare stared out through the front entrance, hoping she looked as if she didn't care. She mentally crossed her fingers. This was it. If King refused to see her it meant she'd failed and Fiona wouldn't get her chance.

It would be just her luck. This last week had been hell, and she was sure that life had a few hard lessons still waiting for her. She darted a look to the elevators. They didn't seem that far away...

'You can go up. Fifteenth floor.' The woman sounded surprised the words were coming from her own mouth. 'Take the elevator on the left, Lady Macbeth.'

In any other circumstances Clare would have laughed at the woman's amazement. 'Thank you.' Her voice was tight.

Had King anticipated this eventuality the other night—that she'd turn up again? His rejection of her invitation on Saturday night might have meant that he didn't want the game to end so soon. Or that he was going to play by his own rules. Her stomach clenched tight. What was she getting herself into?

CHAPTER SIX

CLARE rode the elevator up, straightening her hair and clothes, her heart pounding in her chest and her lips tingling with anticipation.

The chime rang. She hesitated. Did everyone do so much for their siblings or was she being over-protective? No matter what, though, she knew she couldn't leave Fiona hanging in limbo. She flicked the top two buttons of her blouse undone and prayed King was going to be more pliable and accepting today.

The doors of the lift opened.

The rose-painted walls were adorned with oil paint-ings, and plush cream carpet lined the floor. A richly upholstered floral lounge suite surrounded a mahogany coffee table and ferns dotted the room. The pots of foliage flanked each of the three secretaries' desks, lined up against the wall directly in front of Clare, strategically placed to greet visitors, without letting any slip by unnoticed.

Clare took a deep breath. Her entire apartment could fit into this room with heaps of space to spare. It was a great example of big business wasting valu-able cash for appearances' sake.

Clare sucked in her breath and straightened. King

had appropriated all this by stealing businesses, chopping them into little pieces and selling them off to the highest bidder. A shiver ran down her spine. It was the perfect job for him.

The secretary on the left side of the room looked up and smiled. Her name was announced in bronze on the block of wood in front of her. 'He's expecting you.' She pointed to a doorway behind her. 'Lady Macbeth.'

'Thank you, Freda.' Clare nodded to the woman and her cheeks annoyingly heated. She ought to make King suffer slowly and embarrassingly for putting her through all this.

She paused at the double doors leading to his office, willing some strength into her legs. She had to make it work this time.

'It's all right. He's not as bad as everyone makes him out to be.'

Clare darted a glance at his secretary. The older woman smiled. Who was she kidding? Maybe his secretaries were safe from their boss. They could hide behind their glasses and computers, pretending he was perfect, but Clare knew the truth.

She pushed open the doors and strode in, throwing back her shoulders and sucking in her stomach.

He was seated at an impossibly large ebony desk, leaning back in his leather chair, watching her with his dark eyes.

He was as handsome as she remembered.

'M'lady. I knew I'd see you again.'

And as arrogant. Clare clenched her teeth against her body's response to his deep voice, forcing herself to move closer. 'How could I stay away?'

'My thoughts exactly.' He swung out of his chair and met her halfway. 'Care for a drink?'

'Love one.' Clare managed a smile, pushing down the ache deep in her stomach. His dusky grey trousers were expertly tailored, fitting snugly against his body to perfection. His white shirt framed his wide chest, assuring Clare that he was as well built as she'd imagined.

'I know this lovely little café, just round the corner.'

Clare had something a lot stronger in mind, but nodded. 'Fine.'

King snatched his jacket off the back of a chair, slung it over a shoulder and reduced the distance between them at a rate that made Clare swing back towards the door.

King's hand rested in the small of her back, branding her. The heat seared her skin, her blood and her mind. How could he have not taken her home?

He yanked open his door with a flourish. Freda had obviously not been expecting him. She was frozen, nail file in hand.

His glare was icy. 'Mrs Thompson. Just popping out. I'll be back in an hour.'

The secretary opened her mouth. Nothing came out.

*   *   *

The café had a terracotta floor that was jammed with small round tables, littered with chairs, people and waitresses. The aroma of freshly ground coffee beans
and hot pastries invaded Clare's senses.

King led her to a table in a corner and helped her into a seat.

Clare stared King in the face. 'How did you know I'd be back?'

'With all the trouble you went to Saturday night, I'd be very surprised if you'd let me go that easily.'

Her stomach tightened. 'And what trouble would that be?' If he knew, then she'd walked into a lot more than another bout with King, more like a trap!

'The dress, the hair, that divine allure you were radiating.'

She relaxed. 'And I'm not now?'

'No, you're more serious today.' His eyes travelled over her sensible business shoes, up her grey trousers, over her white blouse, resting on her cleavage and the lace of her bra, just visible. His attention finally wandered back to meet her eyes.

'Really? Am I?'

'Yes.' He leant towards her. 'I like your hair down.'

Clare hadn't even thought about her hair. She touched it absently. It probably looked wild from running her hand through it all morning in frustration.

'Are you going to tell me what your game is?'

'No.' She smiled. If luck went her way, he wouldn't realise what she was up to until it was too late.

A waitress wove her way between the tables to them. 'What would you like?' she barked.

Clare jumped in. She knew this one. 'Coffee—black, one sugar—for the gentleman. Tea, white with two, for me.'

The waitress scribbled on her pad. 'That's all?'

'And I'll have a blueberry muffin.'

'And you, sir? Do you want a muffin, too?'

'Yes.' King eyed Clare carefully.

Clare watched the waitress wend her way around the tables back to the kitchen. She folded her arms on the table. 'Do I surprise you?'

'Always.'

'I find that hard to believe. What with being nominated for the Most Eligible Bachelor Award you must find women falling over you all the time.'

He raised an eyebrow. 'Not that I know of. Though I have received a lot of calls since the announcement.' King sobered. 'From all sorts of women I don't know. There was this one woman, my secretary was telling me, who rang ten times. I just hope it doesn't get any worse once the pictures are published next week.'

Her stomach clenched tight. How easily he dismissed her sister... 'Call any of them back?' She could just imagine these women being a real boost for his already inflated ego, like pouring kerosene on a flaming bushfire.

'No. I like to choose my own women.' He raked her with his eyes.

Clare stared him straight in the face, refusing to blush under his scrutiny. 'What if they choose you?'

'Takes two to tango.'

'Excuse me, sir?' a male voice interrupted.

Clare looked up. Mark's assistant, John, stood beside them, looking uncomfortable. *He'd taken her to his usual haunt.* She stared at the condiments on the table, fighting with the slight to her ego at the thought that he brought all his women here.

'Your mobile's turned off.'

'I know.' King's voice was clipped. 'That's because I don't want any interruptions.'

John shuffled his feet. 'A gentleman called from Witherbys. Says he couldn't get onto the number you gave him. Wants you to call him back. He said you instructed him it was high priority.'

Clare watched Mark swallow hard and glance at her briefly, then back to John. 'I'll ring him when I'm ready.' The tone of King's voice was obviously a dismissal.

John turned slowly, his eyes cast down, his mouth pulled thin. Clare felt for him as she would for a puppy getting a slap from its owner for bringing his shoes to him, chew-marks and all.

'Sorry about that.' King leant close to her. 'Business just doesn't let me go sometimes.'

'I know what you mean.' Clare stood up. 'Just going to freshen up.' She sauntered off, scouring her brain for the line of business Witherbys was in. It was crazy, but she felt that it had something to do with her—it would explain King's castigation of John.

The restroom door swung closed behind her. Clare punched the numbers on her mobile for enquiries and was connected.

'Witherby Investigations, how may I direct your call?'

'Freda Thompson,' she rattled off the top of her head. 'I'm ringing on behalf of Mark King. He asked me to check if you had anything yet.'

'Just one moment, I'll put you through to Mr Roberts.'

A man came on the line. 'I assumed Mr King wanted to keep this private?'

'Yes, I'm his *private* secretary. He asks me to deal with all delicate matters.' She prayed he'd take her at her word and not ask her any sticky questions she'd have no chance at answering.

'I understand,' he said knowingly. 'This Clare Harrison is pretty clear-cut.'

Her heart jumped to her throat.

'Her father ran off with another woman when she was ten, shunning the family, as far as I can make out. Real tenacious woman—bought out a chunk of a transport company with an inheritance. Word is she slept her way into a very cosy price.'

Clare stifled a retort.

'Boyfriends by the dozens up until two years ago. For all purposes she appears to use them and lose them.'

'Thank you.' Clare rang off, trying to swallow her uneasiness. *He knew who she was!* Her mind struggled with the fact that he knew, but was continuing the game.

And investigators!

She covered her mouth. Was there a chance he hadn't made the connection between her and her sister? Did the bastard even remember Fiona's name? Or was she just some nameless boost for his ego that he'd dismissed six weeks ago?

That would explain the investigator assuming she was just another wanton woman after his body or his assets.

Clare stared at her reflection. Her cheeks were flushed and her eyes wide. Not the image she wanted to project for King. She breathed deeply, applying make-up to cover her worry. She could handle this. She had to.

Their order had arrived by the time Clare returned.

'Problem?' King put down his coffee.

'No.' She managed a smile and sat down. She wanted to torture this guy's mind until he didn't know which way was up. She lifted her cup of tea to her lips.

King's dark eyes glittered and he leant closer to

her. 'So, tell me about yourself?' He raised his steaming coffee to his lips, the invitation in his look blatantly obvious.

Her body reacted instantly. Blood coursed to parts of it that she would rather ignore. 'Why ask me?' Clare put her cup down. 'I'm sure your investigator will give you your money's worth.'

She had the satisfaction of seeing him choke.

Coffee sloshed onto the table. 'What?'

'But don't believe everything you hear. Those guys are prone to exaggerate to make it sound better, make you feel like you got your money's worth.'

King dabbed at the spilt coffee with a serviette. 'Which part would they colour, do you suppose?' He recovered quickly. He left the sodden napkin and yanked his mobile from his belt, stabbing numbers, his brow furrowed.

'I'll leave that up to you to decide.' She raised her eyebrows mockingly at him. 'I wouldn't want to ruin it for you.'

King eyed her suspiciously. 'Witherbys? It's Mark King.' He darted a glance at her and she raised her eyebrows sweetly. 'What have you got for me?' There was a pause. 'You just did? To whom?' Another pause. 'And the report is?'

Clare ate her muffin as innocently as she could manage. There was no point in making life any easier for the guy. If King wanted a mystery to solve, facts weren't going to help.

He flung the mobile on the table and cocked his head. 'You impersonated my secretary.'

She shrugged. 'You know my name.'

'You knew *her* name.'

She shrugged again. 'Saw it on her desk. How long have you known who I am?' And, more importantly, what else did he know about her?

'Mobiles are funny things.'

Clare darted a look at her purse. 'At the dinner…' She should have guessed he'd had something to do with her returned phone, should have known he wouldn't play by anyone else's rules but his own.

King had the nerve to smile. 'What *is* your story?'

'Didn't you listen to Witherbys? I've come from a broken home, been popular with the boys and climbed up a ladder of bodies to the top.' She took a sip of her tea.

'Do you always believe what you're told?'

'Me? No.' She always preferred to find out the facts herself, but sometimes that was impractical.

'Neither do I. I put everything through a filter.'

Clare raised an eyebrow. 'And where does this filter reside—your head, heart, wallet or loins?'

King laughed. 'You're one crazy lady.'

She stifled the uprising in the pit of her belly. 'Do I take that as a compliment?' This guy was a charmer, and she had to be careful. Other guys were easy to peg, she knew what they wanted, but this guy was different.

'Take it however you want to.' His tone was light. 'But let me take you to dinner.'

At last! 'You'd be a fool to let me out of your sight.' She rose slowly, wiping the creases out of her trousers with long sensual movements that had King mesmerised.

'Where are you going?' His smile faltered.

'I have work to do. You can pick me up at eight at my place.'

'And where is your place?'

Clare smiled and turned. Let that be his next challenge—to come to her place. She'd have him then. Just a simple excuse, invite him in, and— whammy—Fiona gets her chance.

CHAPTER SEVEN

'I DON'T get it, sir.'

Mark wasn't surprised to find John waiting out-side the café. He didn't falter. He strode along the footpath, his assistant keeping up beside him. 'What?'

'She's one of the partners of Trans-Inter.'

'And?' Mark's mind careered off on how delight-fully intriguing she was. He hadn't anticipated her turning up at his office dressed so formally. Rather he'd half expected her to be provocatively attired in something as sexy as that gown she'd worn. But surprisingly it hadn't mattered. His body had reacted to her formal office-wear as fiercely as if she'd worn only lace underwear. He slid his hands into his pock-ets. Imagining what she was hiding under her office blouse and grey trousers was just as entertaining as watching her in that slitted gown had been.

John coughed. 'I don't want to speak out of place, sir. But it seems to me you're mixing business with pleasure.'

Mark faltered. He was, but he couldn't stop smil-ing. What pleasure that mixing was! Clare Harrison was a delightful enigma that he was itching to solve.

'And, sir, you said—'

'I know what I said, and it's damned true— I don't expect any of my employees to compromise my company by mixing business with pleasure.' He glared at the man. 'What I said to you still stands. You break this rule and it's on your own head.'

'Yes, sir.'

'And Clare Harrison is the one that started this little liaison—it's her game, not mine.' He rubbed his jaw. And what a game it was.

Silence enveloped them as they walked. Mark could almost feel John chomping at the bit for power. So much like himself at that age. Wanting it all now. No patience. Just the same arrogant cockiness that Mark himself had started with, and with blind faith he'd get there if he tried hard enough, long enough.

They re-entered his building and rode the elevator.

His rule didn't seem to apply in this case, anyhow. What was best for business was the issue, and finding out what Clare was up to was exactly that— though he couldn't trust his employees to have the same dedication.

They probably thought he was pedantic, but he knew what happened when liaisons ran wild in business. His father was testimony to that, running into bankruptcy twice to support his penchant for fine cars and even finer women. And his hired help... More sex symbols than secretaries!

The first time he'd burst into his father's office

when he was a small child still burned inside him. The sultry blonde draped over his father's lap definitely hadn't been his mother, and the lipstick that covered his father's mouth, chin and neck had had nothing to do with business.

A punch in his gut took him back. His father's scolding about manners, the hard shove in his back sending him out through the door...

John exited on the tenth floor.

'Let me know the moment the documents are done for our deal with Frank Bolton.' The sooner he nailed the company, the sooner he'd peg Clare Harrison and what she was after. He knew that he could confront her about it, but the game she was playing seemed far more interesting than Trans-Inter at the moment.

'Yes, sir.' The doors slid closed again.

Mark straightened his tie. The investigator had said she'd slept her way into a good deal. Did that mean she'd used her body to take control of the company?

His stomach turned. Could she have used her body to ensure her status? Was that what she was doing with him? Ensuring she stayed in control by selling off her luscious body to him? He rubbed his jaw. Interesting. Was he up for the offer?

He couldn't help but smile. When he'd heard Clare was in the building, still using his name for her, he'd figured he was in for a riot. After all, she had to know now that he'd seen Frank and that he was after her company.

Yet she'd floored him. Again. No drama, no hysterics, not a batting of an eyelid over him hooking her partner with a promise of a multi-zero dollar deal. Just that full sultry mouth of hers and those bright blue eyes taunting him with secrets.

He half regretted her missing his tidy little meeting with Frank Bolton—it was just too easy.

The doors opened and he stepped into his office. He stalked over to his secretary. 'Mrs Thompson?'

She looked up and pushed her glasses up along the bridge of her nose. 'Yes?'

'Do I need to remind you that our image is sacred? Do not—' He swallowed hard. 'Kindly do not file your nails while I have anyone in my office or this foyer.' He swept a cursory glance around the empty seats.

'Yes, sir.' She straightened papers on her desk. 'It won't happen again. I just split my nail typing and I had to—'

'Have I made myself clear?' He didn't wait for an answer. He turned on his heel and stalked to his office.

'Mr King?' Mrs Thompson's voice was shrill. 'There's—'

'There's nothing more to say.'

'But—'

Mark pushed open his office doors.

His mother sat in front of his desk with his sister, Jessica. They turned in unison.

Take a good twenty-five years off his mother and he'd be looking at twins—both bleached blondes, green-eyed and lithe. Jess wore hipster jeans and a halter-top; his mother a fine cream linen suit with her string of prized pearls.

'Darling.' His mother stood up.

Mark raised an eyebrow and stalked around his desk. Did a man ever escape his mother? 'To what do I owe this little visit?' He cast a look at Jess, but she was giving nothing away.

His mother didn't miss a beat. 'We've come to invite you to dinner tonight.'

Hell. They could have used the phone. He shrugged off his suit jacket. But then, they knew he'd have wriggled out of it. 'I have other plans.' His mind wandered back to the shape of Clare's body, her piercing eyes and that wicked mouth of hers.

His mother sat down again. 'Surely you can change them? This is for family.'

He stared at the ceiling. How many times had he heard that? His mother often used it to get her own way with him, knowing it was the one thing he couldn't ignore. 'What did you have in mind?'

'A small get-together at my place.' His mother leant forward, rearranging the stationery on his desk.

'Please come.' Jess cast her large moss-green eyes at him. 'For me.'

'That's not fair, Jess.' He couldn't refuse her anything, and she knew it, but he couldn't let Clare fall
through his fingers again. He almost had her pegged.

'What's stopping you, darling?'

'I told you, Mother. I have other plans.'

'Can you get out of them?'

It was more a case of getting into them. His whole
body was itching to find out how much Clare
Harrison had to offer. 'No, I can't.'

'Is it a she?' Jess asked quietly.

'It's business,' he lied.

'Well, I'm sure it can wait, darling. You need
recreation, too.' His mother's eyes glinted.

Clare Harrison was just the recreation he had in
mind. And it would take a lot more than his family
to scare her away, he was sure of it. The idea sent
the blood hurtling through his veins. He couldn't
help but smile—a family party would be the last
thing Clare was expecting.

'I want to get him this time.' Clare threw another
dress onto the bed, juggling the phone in one hand.
'But I've got nothing to wear!'

'Nothing is probably what will work best.'

Clare was sure she could hear her best friend
smiling on the other end of the phone. 'Jeez, thanks.
Why didn't I think of that?'

'Come on, girl. You're taking this all too seriously.' Haley had the nerve to laugh.

'How else could I take it? Look what he did to Fiona without a second thought.'

'I meant what you're wearing. It won't matter. You'll be gorgeous no matter what you wear. He'll be besotted.'

Clare huffed. She didn't want him besotted; she wanted him to face up to his responsibility to her sister and for this to be all over. She picked up her red dress. 'Why aren't you here helping me?'

'Because I'm due to fly out to Europe in about—' there was a pause '—two hours. Tell me again why I do this to myself?'

'Because you can't say no, Haley.' Clare had to smile. Her friend always accepted whatever assignments her company sent her on, from buying Indian silk in Calcutta to tribal shields in Africa.

She'd met Haley at night school. They'd sat next to each other for support, bolstering each other when the endless droning of the lecturers had threatened to put them to sleep. They'd been fast friends since, seeing each other as often as their demanding jobs allowed.

'You're right,' Haley moaned. 'Now, concentrate. What's in your hand now?'

'My short red dress.'

'Perfect. Wear it. I saw some red heels in the back of your cupboard last time I borrowed a dress.'

She probably still had it, too. Clare stared at the scrap of material in her hand. 'But it makes me look like a tart.'

'Isn't that what you want? You want him to think you're offering the lot so he'll fall into your web.'

She sighed. 'Yes, that's what I want.' She hated it when other people were right, especially when she was floundering around in her own insecurities.

'I've got to go. See you in a week.'

Clare listened to the phone's tone for a good minute before she hung up, loath to break the connection and reluctant to lose the excuse for not getting ready. She slipped on the dress, closing her eyes. She didn't want to do this.

She strapped up her heels and looked at herself in the mirror. Her hair was loose, blow-dried to give a carefree, windswept look—though it looked more as if she'd been rolling around in bed. Her make-up was subtle, but the dress itself made up for any decorum there. It was low cut, showing a generous amount of her cleavage, and it hugged her shape, leaving little to the imagination. It stopped a good half a metre short of her knees, which would leave King with no doubt as to her intentions.

She couldn't believe she was wearing it. She'd bought the thing over three years ago for some party, but had never got up the nerve to wear something so audacious—even for Josh.

Haley had helped her through the aftermath of Josh... Clare wished she could be with her now, to hold her hand through this unsavoury situation.

She'd only be wearing the wicked dress on the

landing anyway. As soon as King turned up at the door she'd get him inside. Nobody would see the dress, let alone judge her for it. Except for Mark King and he didn't count.

Clare picked up her glass and sculled the last of the brandy. She eyed the empty glass suspiciously. Confidence should have been oozing through her pores by now.

She took the glass to the kitchen, feeling the warm fluid settle in her belly. She rinsed her glass and leant over to the row of jars. She took another biscuit and bit down forcefully. Something had to quell the mass of nerves fighting deep in her stomach. She took another one for good measure, certain that King was not going to get away tonight.

The doorbell rang.

Clare stiffened. This was it. She walked quickly to the door, rubbing her teeth with a finger, then flicking crumbs from her breasts.

She took a deep calming breath and pasted a welcoming smile on her lips. She wanted this over with and to get out of the dress as quickly as possible. She opened the door.

Her façade faded.

A stranger stood on her doorstep. He was decked out in a black suit and was eyeing her from her head, slowly down her body, to her toes. 'Miss Harrison?' He cleared his throat. 'Mr King sends his apologies. He's caught in a meeting. He asked me to pick you up.'

Clare opened her mouth, but no words came out. This was not the plan!

The men around the table argued fiercely.

King glanced at his watch again. He couldn't believe he was stuck here while the most puzzling woman he'd ever met waited for him. He stared out of the full-height glass windows, his mind running over Clare Harrison's sexy body.

He couldn't wait to discover more about the woman—to test his theories and to kiss that saucy mouth of hers again.

The buzzer sounded. 'Mr King, that package you wanted has arrived.'

'Thank you, Mrs Thompson. I'm sorry, gentlemen.' Mark stood up. 'But I'm afraid I have an important matter to attend to.'

'You can't go, King, not until we make a decision on this.'

Mark raised his eyebrows. 'Our last offer stands. Take it or take the consequences.'

Mark strode from the room. He was charged. He couldn't wait for the next round with Clare.

He glanced at his watch again, then picked up the suit bag draped over Mrs Thompson's desk and strode to the elevator. He wouldn't make Clare wait a minute more than necessary.

The basement was nearly deserted, the air close and heavy. The chauffeur opened the door for Mark. 'Good evening, sir.'

Mark nodded and slid into the back seat. The scent of roses hit him first, then her outfit.

His blood fired at the sight of her.

She was the Scarlet Woman tonight. Her shoes were red, her long legs bare, her hands on the hem of the red dress, trying to drag it closer to her knees. He smiled at her attempt at modesty—it made the effect all the more tempting.

He let his gaze wander upward, taking in the shape of her hips, her waist and her full breasts. The fabric barely held them and their rise and fall mesmerised him.

'Mr King.'

Mark lifted his gaze to her vivid blue eyes. He drank in her defiance, the corners of his mouth twitching at her supposed affront at his perusal.

'Miss Harrison.' He settled himself in his seat and dumped the suit bag on the seat opposite.

Clare placed her hands in her lap.

The limousine moved off and Mark closed the smoked glass partition to the driver. 'I'm sorry to make you wait. I hadn't expected to be kept so late.'

'Yes. I didn't expect this either.'

He cast her a look. There was something different about her tonight, something he couldn't put his finger on. He loosened his tie.

Clare couldn't help but look at him. His strong fingers were working the knot on his tie, loosing it and slipping it off.

She held her breath.

His fingers started on his buttons. The fabric fell open, revealing a well-built chest, scattered lightly with dark curls.

She opened her mouth. Visions of her hands running over his irritatingly attractive body, of how hard and hot he'd feel beneath them, jumped to her mind. 'What are you doing?' She tried to sound calm.

'Getting undressed.'

'I can see that. Why?' She massaged her palms. He couldn't mean to have her, here and now, wham-bam...their bodies entangled, their hands wanton, their lips voracious...

He smiled at her. 'We're running late. I thought I'd change as we travelled. Are you okay with that?' His eyes glinted with challenge.

'Fine. No problem at all.' As long as he kept his hands to himself. It was becoming less of a mystery by the minute as to how her sister had succumbed to the dirty, rotten charmer.

He wrenched his shirt from the confines of his trousers and slipped it from his bronzed shoulders.

She moistened her lips. Yes, his arms were as perfect as the rest of him. 'You work out?' The words slipped from her mouth of their own accord.

'Yes. Nice of you to notice.' His eyes drifted over her body. 'You look pretty good yourself.'

She clamped her mouth closed. Words piled up in her mind—telling him off, telling him to get lost, telling him the truth behind her wicked red dress and that she wanted nothing whatsoever to do with him.

King opened the suit bag and pulled out a crisp white shirt. He slipped one arm into it, then the other, with such deliberate slowness that it was torture.

Clare couldn't tear her eyes away.

He reached for his trousers. She jerked her gaze from the captivating dance of his fingers on his fastenings.

Dark eyes met hers and blood raced to her cheeks at the significance—he'd been watching her watch him. Clare looked to the window, where the city streets passed in a blur.

She heard his zip.

They were on a freeway, and by the scenery she could tell the limousine was heading for the eastern suburbs of Melbourne. The sound of rustling fabric pressed in on her.

Clare knew the eastern freeway well. She visited her mother in the Dandenongs every other weekend, especially now she was unwell again with the flu. Her mother wasn't winning in the battle with her health.

When she heard the zipper again, she darted a look. He was dressed, except his shirt was still hanging loose.

'Are you getting cold feet?'

'Pardon?'

'I didn't expect coyness, Clare.'

Her name on his lips vibrated through her. 'Coy? I thought I was being polite.' She allowed herself to breathe, hoping her hot cheeks didn't give her away.

'Really?'

'You said we were late,' she said calmly. 'I didn't think you wanted to be even later.'

His blazing eyes suggested he was thinking about what they would be like together—wild, passionate, hungry lovemaking. 'I wouldn't have minded.' His deep voice reverberated down her spine.

'Your chauffeur might have.'

'You don't have to worry about him. He's seen all sorts of things.'

'I don't doubt it.' Clare stared out of the window and the limo exited the freeway. 'Where are we?'

King slid towards her on the seat, lifting a hand to her cheek.

Clare flinched.

King hesitated. His eyes bored into hers, then he slowly stroked her cheek, brushing her hair back from her face. 'Alone. We're alone.'

Her heart thudded against her ribs. He was testing her, that was all. She let a smile touch her lips, but avoided looking at the gorgeous expanse of prime male flesh still on show. He could at least have the decency to do his shirt buttons up.

He touched her mouth with the backs of his fingers. She closed her eyes, languishing in the sensation, blocking out the man himself, knowing the game had begun in earnest.

She kissed his strong hand with all the gentleness she could muster, tipping her head and sensually trailing her mouth along his fingers.

The driver tapped on the glass. 'We're here, sir.'

Clare's eyes shot open. 'Where?' She prayed he hadn't brought her to some 'love-nest' of his. Her mind started grappling for excuses.

'My mother's.'

'Your mother's?' She swallowed hard. What on earth was he bringing her here for? She was meant to be another one-night stand, not taken home to Mother! She looked down at her breasts, struggling to escape the skimpy red dress, at the indecent amount of leg she was showing and her striking red stilettos and felt the kind of discomfort she guessed a lap-dancer might feel at the opera. *What had she got herself into?*

CHAPTER EIGHT

MARK took Clare's hand and helped her out of the limousine. He tried not to smile. He'd certainly surprised her—she looked positively put out. 'Problem?'

She flashed him a smile. 'No, of course not. I'm flattered, really.' She smoothed out her dress, looking for all the world as if she was still searching for extra length. She turned towards the house and stiffened.

Mark supposed it did look impressive. The white mansion sprawled in both directions, with a four-car garage at either end. The centre was two-storeyed, with a grand entrance—double leadlight glass doors with full-height side and top panels, all sporting roses in their design. The single-storey annexes on both sides were adorned with windows, all lit, as was the entrance and the long driveway.

Mark buttoned his cuffs with one hand, his suit jacket draped over his arm. 'Like it?'

Clare turned back to him, surprisingly calm. 'It's okay.'

He frowned. It wasn't the house that they'd grown up in as a family, so it meant little to Mark, but his mother went out of her way to make sure it was a grand statement of her lifestyle. She'd be livid to hear it was just 'okay'.

'Don't look so disappointed. A house is a house.' She stepped closer to him and took his jacket. 'Let me.' She held it open for him.

He hesitated. Turning his back on her didn't feel like the sensible thing to do, but there was no way she could hide anything in *that* dress—let alone a knife to stab him in the back before he bought out her company. He turned and slipped his arms into it, shrugging it onto his shoulders. 'Thanks.'

'No problem.' She put her hands on his shoulders and turned him around.

God, she had lovely eyes. He could still see the deep vibrant blue of them, even in the soft illumination of the streetlights. He glanced down to where her fingers were working on the buttons of his shirt. 'What are you doing?'

'What does it look like I'm doing? I'm dressing you.' She darted a glance towards the house. 'I'm not walking in the door dressed like this—' she waved a hand at her attire '—and with you half-dressed.'

'Afraid I might ruin your reputation?'

She hesitated. 'No, I was thinking of your mother.'

Mark's breath caught in his throat. How the hell was he meant to work her out? He caught her hands in his, holding them over his heart.

She glanced up at him and met his gaze, holding it.

He seemed to fill with wanting. There was something in her vivid blue eyes, a fierceness, a hunger, that spoke directly to something deep within him. Where the other women who'd passed through his life had been openly wanton, clear in their designs on him, Clare was different—dangerously so.

Mark dropped her hands. Business was business. 'Ready?'

'As I'll ever be.' Clare was determined not to be a lamb. If King was any indication of what she was walking into with his family, she was going to have one hell of a night. She yanked the fabric up a bit over her breasts—and her hem climbed. She couldn't win. She would just have to do the best she could in a bad situation. And there was no denying it. It was bad.

Putting up with King while he stripped naked in the car would have been enough for one night, but add his family? She'd be more than ready to nail him to the wall tonight!

She cast another look at his mother's residence. It was more than okay. It was extreme. Far bigger and far more grand than she'd ever want. It was in a nice suburb, though, and she liked the way it was nestled amongst the gardens with the wide open sky above. It would be a lovely place to raise children.

The doorbell chimed the toll of Big Ben.

King twined his fingers with hers, kindling a heat

beneath her skin that radiated up her arm and through her body.

The door swung open. A rotund woman dressed in black with a white apron beamed at King. 'Mr King, you're here. Your mother will be so pleased.' She gave Clare a dubious look. 'Come in.'

Clare walked a good pace behind King, careful not to drag on his hand—she'd hate for him to think she was scared. She wasn't, but she was totally unprepared for a family gathering with a man that she loathed.

The house was as extravagant on the inside as the outside. Peach walls encased the large entry, an overly large chandelier hung from the high ceiling, and oil paintings dotted the walls. Clare's red stilettos were conspicuously noisy on the marble tiling.

'Darling, I'm so glad you could come.'

'Hello, Mother.' King's voice was deep and smooth. 'I'd like to present Clare Harrison.' King stood back and let his mother and the whole room see her in all her scarlet glory.

Clare looked down at the petite woman. She wore a cream evening gown, complete with pearls at her ears, around her neck and at her wrists. Her white-blonde hair was pulled up in a regal *coiffure* on her head, and the tilt of her chin and her narrowed eyes left Clare with no doubt at all of her feelings. Clare couldn't have made a bigger contrast had she tried.

King should have just come to her place, as she'd planned. It would be over now, and she wouldn't be standing like some idiot in a room full of strangers in an inappropriate dress. Damn King! He had known this would happen...

It was *all* his fault and she'd make sure he knew it, and regretted it. Clare managed a smile and stepped closer to King. If he wanted to play games...

She put a hand on his arm possessively and met his mother's hard green eyes. 'Lovely to meet you, Mrs King.'

The woman's mouth pulled tight. 'I'm not a King any more. Haven't been for decades. Thank God.' She threw a look at the ceiling. 'Call me Sylvia.'

Clare stared at the woman. The way his mother was looking at her chafed, and she struggled to maintain her control. She wasn't used to being pre-judged, and every inch of her screamed in protest at the injustice of it.

She rubbed King's arm, his muscles hard beneath her hand. 'You have a lovely house, Sylvia.' She looked into the room behind King's mother. It was filled with finely dressed people, antique furniture and the 'help' dressed in black, carrying trays of hors d'oeuvres and drinks. 'And quite a son.' She flashed King a glance.

He raised an eyebrow at her, but his eyes gave nothing away.

'Yes, well...' Sylvia shifted her weight and turned. She signalled a man with a tray of champagne flutes. 'Have a drink and make yourselves...'

She hesitated. Her eyes rested on Clare's hand, still caressing King's arm. 'Mingle. Just mingle and talk.' She managed a tight smile and glided back to her guests.

How could the woman upset her so much? It wasn't as if she wanted King's mother to like her, to fall all over her. She meant nothing to her and King meant *absolutely* nothing to her.

Clare glared at King. 'Are you happy now?'

King looked down at her hand on his arm. 'It takes a bit more than that to satisfy me.'

She dropped her hand. 'I meant, are you happy you've upset your mother?'

'Me?' He widened his eyes. 'I'm acting like the perfect gentleman she thinks I am.' He shot her his wickedly charming smile. 'Don't worry. It takes a lot to upset her. I think she'll live.'

Clare chewed on her inner lip. She knew how precious her own mother was to her, and how disappointed she'd be if she knew what she was doing at this moment.

Clare moved into the room. She shouldn't have played up to King in front of his mum, but she hadn't been able to help herself—being treated as if she wasn't worth the effort had triggered off too many painful memories. She'd done too much, been through too much, to still be treated summarily—even if she had brought it on herself, to some degree, by the game she was playing.

A passing waiter paused, his tray in front of them

and handed them both a glass of pink bubbly champagne.

King held his flute up to hers. 'What shall we drink to?'

'How about success?' She couldn't wait to see his face after she presented her slighted sister to him, and if her sister didn't drive home to the jerk what a womanising bastard he was, she'd be there to press the point.

'Success in what, exactly?' His voice was deeply provocative and his eyes travelled over her breasts.

She looked away from him. He was so transparent, but then, his attraction to her was the whole point. 'Business, of course,' she said contrarily.

'Do you ever mix business and pleasure?'

'Never. Do you?' She already knew the answer. She'd read enough about him to know he kept the strictest guidelines for himself. The gossip around was that he insisted on the same for his employees, with everyone in his employ keeping their minds firmly on the job.

'Not usually.' King's voice lowered. 'But I'm willing to make exceptions.'

She cast him a dubious look. 'To success, then, in all our little ventures.' And in hers in particular. The sooner the better, as far as she was concerned.

She smiled and tapped the side of his glass with hers. Yes, success would be sweet tonight.

King slipped a hand around her waist and steered

her to the far end of the room. 'I wanted to ask you about your company.'

'Well, it's not mine—not all of it.' She looked over his shoulder, looking for a distraction, loath to talk about her company with him. The last thing she needed was King sticking his nose in her personal life—or, worse, her business one.

'You run it, though?'

'Yes.' Clare couldn't help but smile. She was proud of what she'd done with the place since Frank had handed her the reins, but she couldn't have done so well if Frank hadn't had the utmost confidence in her.

'How did you manage that position?'

'I took advantage of the situation at exactly the right time.' If Frank had kept his personal life together after his wife left Clare wouldn't have come so far, so quickly. But if she could have changed Frank's wife's mind about the divorce she would have. Frank was only half the man without his wife, as though she'd taken a large chunk of him as well as the house, car and various assets.

'That was opportunistic of you.'

'Yes, but canny.' She sipped the sweet liquid. Frank hadn't ever complained about the arrangement—who would? Anyone would be thrilled to pick up the dividends while someone else did the work.

'Very.' King's voice was deeply suggestive.

Clare clenched her toes and raised her eyes to

meet his. If only she could read his mind, but then, she had a fair idea what would be going on—or off—in it, and it wouldn't have much to do with business.

King took a gulp of his champagne. 'Do you ever have problems with your own ethics versus the company?'

'That's kind of deep.' Clare took a crouton from a passing tray and dipped it into a hot, rich cheese.

'Humour me,' Mark demanded quietly, 'I'm interested.'

She shrugged. 'The company comes first.' Was he testing the water to see how committed she was to her work before involving himself with her? He'd be the first to be so careful. 'Always has. Always will.'

King's eyes darkened.

Clare popped the tangy morsel into her mouth and licked her fingers, searching the room for one of the waiters for a serviette. It didn't serve as much of a distraction. She knew she was losing King. She was being too honest, and it was plain he was after a hot affair with a besotted woman, not a career woman with responsibilities.

She turned back to him, concentrating on getting every scrap of warm, melted cheese from her fingers as slowly and suggestively as she could. She ran her tongue slowly up and down her fingers, meeting King's stormy eyes, challenging him to keep his control.

She wet her lips before tackling the next finger.

She had him mesmerised.

His eyes followed her tongue.

Every nerve in her body was tuned to the power of seduction, her eyes intent on his, her mind screaming her folly at playing with fire.

'Son. I want a word!' King's mother grabbed his arm.

Clare straightened and looked away. She didn't know whether to laugh or cry at being caught by his mother. She took a gulp of her drink. Upsetting his mother was the last thing she'd intended to do; the poor woman looked enough of a stress case without Clare pushing her over the edge.

'Okay.' King's voice was deep and husky. He cleared his throat, a red flush creeping up his neck. 'Yes, of course.'

Clare watched them move off, careful not to miss King's formidable frame following his mother's small one through a swinging white door. If he was any other man she'd find him delectable.

She couldn't help but smile. If only she could be a fly on the wall in there and watch King's mother chewing the great Mark King's ear off for being far too familiar in front of her guests. She could almost hear her words— *It just won't do.*

'Hello,' a warm young voice said.

Clare turned. The white-blonde was young and smiling, her face oddly familiar.

'I'm Jess—Mark's sister. Don't mind my mother.

She's just a fanatic perfectionist. And a control freak.' The girl shrugged. 'You'll get used to her.'

Clare shot her a warm smile. 'Thanks.'

'You've come with Mark?' Jess looked at her hands.

'Yes, I have,' Clare said carefully. She wasn't sure what to say. She couldn't remember a time when she'd been so baffled as to what she should do next.

'And you like him? Have you known him long?' She sucked in a breath. 'Why I ask is because my friend really likes him. You may have met her. Her name is Sasha.'

Clare nodded. She was starting to get the gist of where this conversation was heading. 'And you'd like me to back off?'

'Only if you aren't *serious*-serious.' She stared her in the eye. 'I wouldn't stand in the way of true love, and all. So…?'

Clare swallowed. 'I won't be going anywhere.'

Jess broke into a smile. 'You love him, don't you?' Jess glanced to the door where her brother and mother had exited. 'I knew it! I can *so* tell. I may be young but I'm not blind. I've watched enough TV to know *that* look, and I just wanted to tell you that I like you. And it's okay with me—truly.'

Clare opened her mouth. And closed it. What could she say to the girl?

'Mother wants someone a little more classy—' Jess stepped back and perused Clare's dress. 'But I think you've got a style and spunk all of your own. Mark needs that. He's had too many cookie-cutter cutey-pies. He needs a real woman.' She smiled, her green eyes glinting. 'That's you.'

'Thanks. I think.' Clare shifted awkwardly. This was the weirdest situation she'd ever landed herself in!

Jess moved off suddenly. 'Gotta go. Someone's just spilt wine on Mother's brand-new rug!'

Clare watched Jess dive into the crowd, thankful she didn't have to respond to Mark's sister. She let out a long breath, wishing she could stand quietly off in the corner. But her attire didn't lend itself to being unobtrusive.

The guests were staring at her and the reality of her display sank in. She shifted her weight on her heels, looking at the door King had left through. She was wasting time. They'd made an appearance. It was time King took her home and then she could get it over with.

Clare's stomach ached.

Her feet moved of their own volition, following the path King's had taken. She didn't care what King's relationship was with his mother, or what sort of problems she'd caused him by turning up. It was none of her concern.

The kitchen was mayhem. Three chefs and several assistants were bustling around the large room. It looked as though Sylvia's idea of a party involved a full sit-down dinner—there was enough food to feed an army.

'What?' a chef barked.

'Sylvia?' Clare mouthed over the din. The man pointed to another swinging door to the left and she pushed through it.

The dining room was enormous. A grand mahogany table, looking to seat over forty people, was decked out to perfection with all the cutlery, fine bone china and glassware a hotel could ever wish for. But there was no King.

There were several other doors. Clare listened at each one until she heard Sylvia's voice.

'How could you bring someone who looks like that here, for goodness' sakes? You knew who'd be here tonight. For Pete's sake, she looks like you picked her up on some street corner in St Kilda.'

'Appearances aren't everything.' King's voice sounded surprisingly calm.

'How can you say that? Listen to yourself.' She let out an exaggerated sigh. 'She's not pregnant, is she?'

Clare stiffened.

Mark coughed as though his champagne had gone down the wrong way. 'What?'

'Well, why else would you bring *her*?'

'She interests me.'

'What about Sasha?'

'*What* about Sasha?' King's voice was strained.

'You're not blind. The girl's in love with you. She'd be better for you than that, that—'

Clare held her breath. She didn't want to hear. This woman knew nothing about her, absolutely nothing. She was going by looks alone, and Clare knew exactly where that would leave her.

'Don't say it, Mother. Don't even think it. She's one very intriguing woman that I want to get to know a lot better.'

'Be careful. You know what that sort of girl is after.'

Clare's cheeks burnt. She pushed open the door, her feet moving of their own accord, her mind filling with retorts.

'And what is that, Sylvia?' Clare blurted. She wanted to hear what his mother thought was worse than what King had done to her sister. She could feel the indignation rising like a storm inside her. Sylvia had no idea what she'd been through, what she'd sacrificed for her family, and she had no right to air her hasty assumptions...

'Eavesdropping too! What sort of manners is that?'

Clare opened her mouth and closed it. What could she say? The situation was going from bad to worse and the only thing she could think was *A closed mouth gathers no foot.*

King stepped between them. 'Will you excuse us a moment, Mother?'

'Gladly.' His mother tipped her nose in the air and turned with a swish of cloth.

Mark faced Clare, catching her hands and holding them to his chest. 'I'm sorry, Clare. You didn't deserve that.'

Her belly clenched. 'She had no right to say I'm a tramp.' She felt an annoying sting behind her eyes.

'I know. But does it matter to you what she thinks?' He stared down at her mouth.

Clare moistened her lips instinctively.

His eyes darkened.

Her heart slammed against her ribs.

Mark took her by the shoulders, his face stern, as though he were having a war with himself and losing. His fingers dug into her skin and he pushed her backwards, up against the wall, wrapping his arms around her, crushing his mouth to hers.

His lips were hard and punishing, but her blood fired at his passionate hunger. She kissed him back, her tongue urging him on, her hands running up his back, digging her fingers into his jacket.

Why was he wearing so much? She slipped her hands down and under, catching his shirt and tugging it free.

His skin was hot and her body ached. The power of him took hold of her. It was like breathing the same air, and she wanted more of him. Much more.

He ran a hand up under her arm, down the swell of her breast, the side of her waist, her hip and leg, then up again. His hand climbed her thigh and cupped her bottom.

He kissed her chin, her cheek, her jawline, then he moved his hot mouth down her neck, sending eruptions of pure delight coursing through her.

She ran a hand through his dark hair, caressing the back of his neck. She wanted to groan her lust for him, but the sound caught in her throat at the click of the door. Clare opened her eyes. What was she doing? Here? Now? With *him*!

King pulled her closer to him, his desire for her evident. His lips trailed a hot path down her neck.

Wide hurt eyes met Clare's. 'Sasha!'

King froze.

Clare slid her hand from his shirt, her other hand dropping from his back. She straightened.

'What are you doing with *her*?' Sasha's voice was shrill. 'I thought… We—'

King dropped his hands from Clare's body and turned. 'Sasha.' His voice was soft, gentle. 'You've got the wrong idea.'

Sasha turned on her heel and flew out of the room.

Clare held her breath. Her body was tingling crazily, her hands yearning to rip King's clothes off and kiss his maddeningly sexy lips. What had he done to her?

'I have to go after her.'

An unfamiliar surge of emotion welled up in her throat, of anger and disgust all rolled into one. 'What exactly is your relationship with her?' She needed to hear so her body would remember what a horrible man he was.

'There is no relationship.'

Case proven. 'Then why—?'

'She's young and has taken things the wrong way.' He touched her shoulder, letting his hand trail down her skin to her wrist before dragging her to him.

Like Fiona had taken their lovemaking to mean so much more than it obviously had meant to him?

He brushed his lips over hers lightly. 'Later?'

Clare nodded. She shouldn't have encouraged him. It was like toying with a bear, especially when she was so keen to be damned edible.

She clenched a fist and watched him leave. If she were a man she would just deck the guy and get on with it—not pussyfoot around with him like this. It was time for business.

She just had to survive the trip back to her place without losing her control, her clothes and her self-respect. And why, she wanted to know, were the good lovers all bastards?

Mark found Sasha outside. The fountain was bubbling gently and the garden lights created a softness in the grounds. His mother always insisted on the best, and the landscaped garden was no exception. Nor was her taste in suitable women for him to date.

He descended the stairs from the raised courtyard, passed through an arch of flowering jasmine and strode down one of the maze of tiled pathways that wove through the garden. He caught the scent of lavender. Even in the dim light he could see the expert combination of colour the gardener had effected by combining the deep greens of unusually-shaped topiaries with roses, lavender and an array of what looked like wildflowers.

Sasha stood with her back to him. Her full-length black evening gown made her appear more mature, as did her hair piled high atop her head. But he wasn't fooled.

'What's going on, Sasha? I've gone out of my way to make it clear that I have no intention—'

'I didn't expect you to bring her *here*.' Her voice was tight. She turned to face him. Her eyes were bright and her cheeks flushed.

'It was a last-minute decision.' He caught himself. He didn't have to explain anything to her. 'But, Sasha, we've gone out once and—'

'Did you see what she was wearing?'

'Yes. I did.' He couldn't help but smile. He didn't mind shocking his mother and her guests. Clare was right. His life had become too organised—too controlled.

'I would never dream of compromising myself or your family by wearing something like that.'

Mark sighed. He'd thought he'd been so careful with Sasha. He didn't want any more strings in his life. All he'd wanted was a pretty woman to go with him to one function without deciding she owned him. 'Sasha, I want to make it clear. There is nothing between us.'

She cast him a wary glance. 'Of course not.' She laughed. 'Though I would appreciate the chance,' she said more seriously, gazing up at him.

'As I've said before. You're too nice for me.' The last thing he wanted to do was hurt her feelings. She was important to his sister and Jess would never forgive him if he messed this up. They had to be friends.

Sasha looked down at her hands. She was twisting a ring on her finger, her movements erratic. 'And *she's* not too nice?'

'No, she's not.' His mind slipped off on a delightful tangent—exploring how wicked Clare could be. His blood heated at the thought and he couldn't wait to find out if he was right about her.

Sasha looked up at him. 'Well, at the very least you have to return the favour.' She plucked a wildflower from the garden.

'What favour?'

'I accompanied you to that charity dinner. You have to accompany me to a friend's party. It's actually a friend of a friend, but everyone is going to be there.'

Mark rubbed his jaw. He didn't want to feed Sasha's fancy, but he did owe her one. 'Sure. But on the strict basis that there are no strings attached.' The words had a hollow ring. It was plain that Sasha was already weaving her strings. He wasn't blind—

she probably had Jess's blessing and her advice as to how to entrap him. Tonight was probably all a set-up. But they hadn't counted on Clare.

Sasha smiled. 'I wouldn't dream of it.'

Mark looked her over carefully. He was going to have to watch his step. Maybe he could work out some way to show her he wasn't for her.

He glanced towards the house and saw Clare's silhouette against the window. He'd recognise her shape anywhere. He'd all but memorised every inch of her in that dress.

An intensity flowed through him at the thought of Clare. God, he wanted to be close to her. He itched to get under her skin like she had with him, and he wanted her to ache for him until it was unbearable, until she begged for his kiss, his touch, for all of him.

'Call me,' he offered Sasha.

He strode back to the house, his heart thumping madly against his ribs, his blood singing for the woman who waited for him. He'd had enough of his mother's party. It was time to find out exactly how far Clare Harrison took her dedication to her company.

CHAPTER NINE

BLOCKHEAD. Dimwit. Schmuck.

Clare tried to keep her hand steady as she thrust the key into the lock. The trip home in King's limousine had been all hands and lips, and it had been all she could do to remain in control of herself, let alone the situation. She shouldn't have primed him at the party. She should have predicted what the trip would be like after seducing him. What his chauffeur thought, she had no idea...

She took out her keys and jangled them loudly, praying Fiona was ready. Fiona knew what to do as long as she didn't lose her nerve—King was going to get exactly what was coming to him.

She'd never have to put up with him, his touch, his kiss again. Her lips tingled. Maybe she could kiss him one last time to prime him for the finale.

'You live alone?' His voice was a bare whisper in her ear as his body pressed close against her back, his arms sliding around her and slipping over the fabric on her stomach. He kissed her neck, working his hot lips along her throat.

Her body ached at his touch. 'Do you?' Clare countered softly, willing her body to behave.

'Yes. On and off.'

Clare pushed the door open and they stepped as one into the entry. No sooner were they were inside than his lips were claiming hers again, tasting her softness, exciting her blood.

She couldn't help but kiss back—she told herself the plan depended on him being convinced. Besides, his kiss was so warm, so dreamy, so perfect. She ran her hands up his chest and over his shoulders, shrugging his jacket off.

His lips danced magically over hers and his hands ran down the back of her dress and up again, to clasp her zipper.

She broke the kiss. 'Not yet.' She touched his arms and guided them back to her waist.

She opened his shirt, button by button, gazing into his steamy grey eyes. One of his hands wandered up her ribs to the swell of her breast and she gasped as ripples of sensation coursed through her at his touch.

Clare broke away and sucked in a deep breath, fighting the urges threatening to smother her reasoning. She took King's hand firmly and led him into her room. She couldn't afford to hesitate, to look into his stormy eyes again. He was a womaniser, a real ladies' man, and she could see why, feel why, in every nerve of her body. He knew the magic way to a woman's heart.

She tasted his mouth, languishing in one last kiss. She wanted the moment to last for ever, to live in the illusion that he was someone else, someone she was allowed to feel for, someone who felt for her. But he wasn't. And she had to make it right for Fiona.

King raised his hand and pushed the hair out of her face, his eyes glittering with a promise she'd never know.

She backed away.

'Where are you—?'

'Back in a minute.' Clare pasted what she hoped looked like a provocative smile on her face and slipped out through the door.

Fiona was waiting.

'He's in—' Clare's voice broke. She cleared her throat and tried to throw off the lust sizzling in her veins. 'In there. You can tell him exactly what you want.'

'Do you think there's any hope of a relationship?'

Clare stared at her sister, wide-eyed. 'No.' Mark King wouldn't be into a long-term relationship with her sweet, unassuming sister. From what she knew of him Clare couldn't see him in a long-term relationship, full-stop—she figured he'd still be chasing skirts at eighty.

Fiona stepped inside.

Clare held her breath, biting her lip. This was it. It would all be over in a couple of seconds and she wouldn't have to play King's game—any game—again.

She could hear nothing but silence and the painful thud of her heart in her chest.

The door flung open and Fiona reappeared. Her eyes were wide and her face ashen. She lunged towards her, slamming the door closed behind her.

Clare stepped forward. 'What happened?' She couldn't understand how she could let him off so quickly, so lightly! 'Surely you could have talked longer—abused the guy or something? I put a lot of effort into getting him here for you.'

'I know, Clare.' Fiona bit her bottom lip, her eyes glazing. 'But that isn't him.'

'What?' Clare shook her head. Maybe King had affected her hearing as well as the rest of her body. 'How can it not be him?'

'I have no idea. That isn't Mark King.' She touched her belly. 'He's not the father of this child.'

CHAPTER TEN

CLARE stood stock still. Her mind was numb. How could he be the wrong guy after everything she'd been through?

They'd researched Mark King. They knew his birthday, his mother's name, his sister's name, his father's name, his whole company's brutal history. Sure, they hadn't had the time to search every business paper in the hopes of a photo of him—it had never been a consideration—but…it had to be him!

'That *is* Mark King.' Clare had been to the charity dinner, his office, his mother's home—they couldn't all be wrong—there was no way they could all be wrong.

She chewed her lip. That left them with the plain fact that Fiona had succumbed to someone else—to a man who was pretending to be King for some insane reason—and she'd done all this for nothing.

Clare sagged against the back of a chair. She'd spent all this time chasing after some stranger for justice while her company was getting sold out from under her. She closed her eyes, feeling the pain seep to her toes. Time she could have spent saving it.

She darted her eyes around her lounge room. It was crazy to doubt his identity, but she couldn't wrench her attention away from Mark's jacket, lying on the floor where she'd dumped it. She took two strides forward, snatched up the jacket and plunged her hand into his pockets, one after another.

'What are you doing?' Fiona's voice was high-pitched, her panic evident. She'd never coped well in stressful situations—she was more the type to throw her hands over her face than confront the danger.

Clare had to admit she wasn't coping much better—every muscle in her body was strung taut, her breath short and laboured, her hands shaking. Her fingers clasped around a thick square wallet and drew it out. She turned it slowly. The soft fine leather was branded in gold with the initials 'MK'.

Clare stabbed a finger towards her room, vividly aware of the seconds speeding past. 'I'm making sure he's who I know he is.'

She flicked the leather open. The wad of cash struck her first. There had to be at least a thousand dollars crammed into the wallet—disposable cash for him, she figured—and a dozen credit cards.

Fiona leant closer. 'He must have one from every bank.' She sighed. 'How rich do you think this guy is?'

'Very.' Clare gave one of the cards a yank. Mark King's name was on it in big bold letters.

'I guess you can fake them,' Fiona whispered.

She yanked out his driver's licence—again *Mark King*, with a photo to match the man in her bedroom. It was stupid to think he was anyone else, but she had to be sure. Things were too weird, especially the way her brain ceased to function rationally where he was involved.

'It *is* him.' Clare shoved the wallet back into the jacket pocket and stared at her bedroom door—the real live Mark King was waiting for her.

Fiona dropped onto a lounge chair. 'Then who was the man I—?' Tears marked her cheeks. 'Oh, God, Clare. He could have been anyone.' She tried to smother a sob. 'What am I going to do now?'

Clare touched her sister's shoulder lightly, then wrapped her arms around her. 'You're not alone. You've got Mum and you've got me. We'll help you, whatever you decide.'

Fiona nodded and lifted her head. 'What are you going to do with that man in there?'

Clare's body buzzed with the notion that she did have the wrong guy waiting for her in her bedroom. A guy who made her feel things she'd never felt before, like the burning desire to tear his clothes off.

'Any suggestions?' Clare had no idea what to do. She'd never considered going through with her seduction. He was meant to be the same Mark King who had bedded down with her sister and shunned her. And at this moment, according to her plan, he should have been confronted with her sister's problem and have accepted his part in her predicament, losing all his ardent attention for Clare. She'd imagined him making an embarrassed hasty exit; as it was, she couldn't see him leaving without a very sticky confrontation of her own.

Her mind drifted. She was sure Mark King would be an experience to remember. His kisses were intoxicating. But, as much as her body ached for the man, it wasn't right.

Her heart lurched. What was she going to say to the guy when she went back in there? It was a wonder he hadn't come rushing out.

'This is all my fault.' Fiona wiped the tears from her eyes. 'He's going to expect you to—' She touched her belly with the flat of her hand.

'I know.' And the thought both thrilled and frightened her. There was a large chunk of her that wanted to throw all caution to the wind and indulge in everything Mark King had to offer.

'Look, you go. Go to Mum's, or something. I'll tell him…' Fiona chewed her lip. 'I'll tell him something.'

'Tell me what?' Mark demanded, striding into the room, straightening his clothes. 'If you two have quite finished, I'd like to know what's going on.'

'Nothing,' Clare managed. She clenched her teeth together, grappling for a reasonable excuse.

Mark advanced. 'What sort of nothing?'

'A family matter has come up. I'm afraid I have to cut our evening short.' Clare mentally crossed her fingers. It sounded okay…

Clare couldn't even look at him. Mark had to know enough about people to know this wasn't right. He had to wonder what it was that had changed things. What he thought of Fiona bursting into the room and staring open-mouthed at him for a good thirty seconds before losing all colour and racing out again, she had no idea.

'It's my fault, really,' Fiona blurted. 'I asked her to—'

'To help her.' Clare shot Fiona a warning look. 'She asked me to help her with a problem.'

Mark eyed her. 'Do you want me to stay?'

Clare hesitated. A yearning ache roiled in the pit of her stomach at the thought of Mark King leaving. She straightened the magazines on the coffee table and picked up the coffee mug left there. It wasn't right. She should just tell him the truth. That she'd researched him, pursued him and seduced him for revenge. She swallowed a wave of nausea. That wasn't an option.

Much as she wanted to scream *yes*, she couldn't. Not given the circumstances. One, he was still the enemy—a different breed of enemy but an enemy all the same. And, two, her sister was in the apartment. Her sister's condition was one issue; the other was that Fiona didn't need to know how desperate Clare was for this guy.

'I'm sorry,' she offered.

'No problem.' Mark grabbed his jacket off a chair, pulled out his mobile and dialled a taxi. 'These things happen. If there's anything I can do—?'

Clare didn't miss the way he balled his fists before shoving them deep into his trouser pockets. What he was thinking of her now, she didn't want to consider. She'd been bold and wanton, an outright tease! 'Thanks, but I think we'll manage.'

Clare closed the door quietly after him, wondering for all she was worth how the heck she'd ended up in this situation. Who on earth would pretend to be someone they weren't—and Mark King, of all people?

Her chest ached. And more importantly, would Mark King want anything to do with her now?

Mark dragged himself out of bed, his bedding twisted and strewn half across the floor. Ridding himself of Clare Harrison wasn't proving easy. She haunted him every time he closed his eyes, the sight of her rousing his body to her mysteries and his mind to her games.

He snatched the phone off the nightstand, surrendering to the inevitable. There was no way he could forget the woman, let her go, until he'd figured her out. He'd find out exactly what life Clare had and how to negotiate around it to make her his.

He caught himself as he dialled John's number. He didn't need to involve his personal assistant. This was the *most* personal.

Mark stomped through his penthouse apartment. The modern black furniture irked him today. The black lounge suite swallowed the light in the room and the crisp white walls were stark. Even the abstract paintings lacked the fire that Clare's place had. What colour she had, what confidence, to have painted the walls blue and red. Like the confidence she had in herself. Why not in him?

The idea that she'd think he couldn't help her out, that she couldn't burden him with her problems... His gut recoiled. He would have to show her what a gentleman he was, prove to her that he was different.

He yanked open a cupboard door and dragged out the *Yellow Pages* phone directory. He'd do this on his own. If Clare Harrison had secrets, he was going to find them.

CHAPTER ELEVEN

CLARE showered, but much as she tried she couldn't remove the tingling awareness that King had awakened in her body. She doused herself with cold water, then leapt from the cubicle and towelled herself warm. The reality was that indulging in thoughts about Mark King wouldn't help save her company.

She dressed in a fawn-coloured linen suit. She did her blouse up slowly, wishing she hadn't got Mark King so incensed. She shook her head. She still had difficulty grasping the fact that King wasn't the guy that had cruelly used her sister.

She tied her hair back and adorned it with an arched piece of shell, plunging an ornate needle through the shell's hole to fix the piece at her nape.

At times like this she wondered what the 'simple life' would be like, with no cares or concerns, then shunned the idea. She'd be bored. She loved a challenge. And what better challenge had there been than taking on Mark King? Even if he was the wrong guy. She shook her head and she slipped her tan shoes on.

She paused. In all the confusion last night one fact had escaped her. She was free to explore this feeling he evoked in her. A sliver of desire coursed through her anew.

But would *he* want to? After that poor excuse he probably wouldn't want anything to do with her. Clare cringed, wondering what else she could have come up with that would have made sense.

Clare grabbed an apple from the fruit bowl and plucked up her keys. She bit into the apple. There was the chance that she might never see the guy again, and the thought made her chest ache.

The office was a hive of activity when Clare arrived. She glanced at her watch, amazed that she was a half-hour late and hadn't even noticed.

'Good morning,' Fiona offered, looking up from her desk. 'I was starting to wonder whether you were going to turn up at all.'

Clare sighed—it was good to see her sister at work, hadn't even thought that she would have beaten her to the office. 'No, I'm fine.' She smiled. 'Good to see you back.'

'I couldn't stand the thought of another day at home. I was bored witless.' Fiona picked up a pen and chewed the end. 'Are you upset about last night?'

Clare shook her head and strode into her office, biting her tongue. She went to the window and stared out. The industrial estate didn't have much of a view and the sides of factory walls didn't do much to distract her from the latest drama in her life.

Fiona followed. '*Are* you going to see him again?'

Clare bit her lip, but she couldn't help but smile. She knew exactly what she was going to do with him if she did. He had the most luscious lips she'd ever kissed and she was all for finding out how they'd feel on her body. 'If he wants to see me.'

'O-kay,' Fiona lilted. 'At least something good has come from this mess. Do you think there's any chance of finding the guy who—?' She broke off, choking on the words.

Clare turned and frowned. 'I can't see how. Without his name…'

Fiona dropped her gaze, staring at her hands again.

Clare wanted to kick herself. Fiona's problems far outweighed Clare's in every way. 'I guess you could hang out where you met him,' she suggested. 'Maybe he goes there often. It was in the local coffee shop, wasn't it?'

'Yes.' Fiona brightened. She glanced at her watch.

'Sure.' Clare touched her sister on the shoulder. 'It's time for a cup of tea. Bring me back a Lamington with cream.'

'Thanks. Oh, and here.' Fiona handed Clare a wad of paper. 'These are your messages.'

Her little sister cast her a hopeful smile and closed the door to her office. Clare took a deep breath. She wished she could run off and discover where Mark stood now, but knew she would have to wait. Her company held a higher priority than rushing into another awkward situation where she'd have to confess her stupid ploy.

Clare flicked through the messages. All the banks had responded and all had declined a loan on the grounds of insufficient collateral. Without putting up her mother's house as well as her apartment she had no hope of coming close to any bank's requirements. And she wouldn't do that for the world. She couldn't risk her mother's security for the chance to buy the company.

She closed her eyes and imagined fleetingly what it would have been like to be her own boss, totally and utterly, with no one to answer to, no one to order you around and no one to sell out your company from under you.

A knock on the door broke her reverie.

Clare looked up from her desk. 'Come in.'

The door opened. Mark King stood in the doorway. He looked incredible. The dark blue designer suit complemented his olive skin. His white silk shirt and a turquoise tie only enhanced the effect. His grim set jaw was clean-shaven. His dark eyes impaled her. 'Miss Harrison.'

'Mr King.' Clare stood up. She had no idea how to approach him. He was no longer her sister's user. He was no longer a stranger. She'd made sure of that. What he thought of her at the moment was what was important.

'I wanted to talk about last night.' His voice resonated through her.

'Me too.' She cleared her throat. 'Look, Fiona—'

Mark put up a hand. 'No need to explain.' He moved closer to her, not taking his dark eyes off her.

Her pulse responded. 'Yes, there is. I don't want you to think—' Clare's breath caught in her throat.

Mark reduced the distance between them.

She was drawn to his stormy eyes, fiercely determined, glittering with a smouldering flame that made silent promises to her body. 'I want you to know that—' she started.

He raised his hand slowly and touched his fingers against her lips. 'I said it's okay.'

A shiver of desire ran through her, and all thoughts deserted her mind. Clare stared up at his mouth, willing him to take hers, revive the passion she'd had in his arms.

Mark bent his head and the touch of his lips on hers was painfully gentle as his warm mouth moved over hers reverently, caressing and exploring, igniting her blood.

He wrapped his arms around her, encasing her in his strength, the heat of his body emanating from him like a beacon to hers.

Clare couldn't resist. She could barely control the pounding need that drummed deep within her. She kissed him back, inciting him to a faster pace, plundering his mouth with the passion she wanted to share with him.

She trailed kisses along his strong jaw and downward, breathing hot kisses where his pulse beat his desire for her.

Mark groaned. 'Clare.'

It felt so good to hear him say her name again. And this time she was allowed to embrace the emotions he evoked. This time she could plunge into the deep end.

The phone rang.

Clare rubbed her hands up his shirt, feeling every muscle ripple under her touch with delight, cursing the fact that she couldn't ignore the call—it might be a bank. 'I have to get that. My secretary is out.'

Mark kissed her earlobe. 'I noticed.'

She fumbled for the receiver, one hand wandering up to Mark's neck, brushing over his freshly shaven face, over his ear and through his thick black hair. 'Clare Harrison.'

'Hi, Clare. It's me, Paul. I hope everything went as planned the other night.'

Clare stiffened. She covered the receiver. 'Business.' She edged out of Mark's embrace, giving herself a good two metres, offering him a consolatory smile. 'Yes?'

'I'm calling in that favour, okay?'

'Your timing's not so good.' She stared into Mark's deep grey eyes. The last thing she wanted to do was waste an evening with her cousin when she could be enjoying Mark's company and more. Mark perused her slowly, undressing her with his eyes, and her body tingled in anticipation.

'Tonight. No buts. This is the big one. Everyone will be there. You've got to come, Clare. You promised.'

Clare could imagine doing far more interesting things with Mark King tonight, all night. But a promise was a promise, and Paul had helped her gatecrash King's charity gala. 'All right.'

'I'll pick you up at eight. Wear something sexy.'

'Okay.' But not her red dress—never again! She rang off, moving closer to Mark. Well, maybe she'd make an exception for Mark...as long as they didn't leave the bedroom.

'Problem?'

'No.' She cleared her throat. 'No, everything's fine.' She rubbed her body up against his and wrapped her arms around him.

His lips recaptured hers. Her body lurched at his hot, drugging exploration and she opened herself to him and languished in his mastery.

She trailed her hands up his chest, plucking his buttons undone to feel his hard warm body under her fingertips.

He broke the kiss and dragged in a deep, long breath. 'I have to go. Can I call you?' He brushed his lips against her forehead, tracing the shape of her face with his thumb and forefinger.

'Definitely.' She moved her hands lazily to his buttons, dressing him. 'But I'm busy tonight.'

'Me, too.' He hesitated. 'Business.' His eyes probed hers.

Clare nodded. 'Ditto.' The last thing she needed was to advertise she was going out with another man, even though it was Paul. She had to keep the two of them away from each other—that way, what she'd got up to at the charity dinner, and why, would stay as it should—a secret.

'See you.' He ran his eyes over her again, as though committing her to memory. He grasped the door handle and shot her his devastating smile.

Clare's heart lurched. 'Yes.' She'd be seeing a lot more of Mark King. Right after she'd saved her business.

CHAPTER TWELVE

MARK closed the office door behind him and straightened his tie. There was no way he could fathom what Clare was about. But whatever was going on, he'd find out.

He'd called several investigators earlier, and hired them all. He didn't care about cost. He was itching for answers—as soon as he could get them.

'I'm sorry. I didn't know you were here.' A woman's voice, small and weak.

Mark turned. Clare's little sister sat at the front desk, her eyes red. 'I didn't know you worked here,' he offered as he scanned the room, her desk, her. Nothing jumped out as to why she would be crying. 'I'm sorry. I don't think I caught your name last night.'

'Fiona.' She sniffled into a handkerchief. 'Don't mind me.' She picked up a file and stared blankly at it.

'Problem?'

'No,' she said quickly. 'Yes!' Tears spilled from her eyes. 'A big one.'

Mark didn't hesitate. He moved around the desk and crouched in front of her. He was used to Jess's tears and being a shoulder to cry on. 'You want to talk about it? Should I get Clare for you?'

She shook her head. 'It won't help. There's nothing she can do. There's nothing anyone can do.'

'Try me.' Mark waited expectantly. It piqued his curiosity as to what exactly it was that was beyond Clare's ability to solve for her sister. To all intents and purposes she came across as Superwoman, capable of doing anything she put her mind to.

Fiona stared at him, her bottom lip quivering. 'I met this man.' She blew her nose into the handkerchief. 'And we…and I—and I'm pregnant.'

Mark couldn't help but dart his eyes to where her hand lay protectively on her stomach. 'Let me guess. He got the shock of his life and disappeared?'

Fiona shook her head. 'Not really. We can't even find him to tell him.'

He smiled. 'I find that hard to believe. I can give you the number of an investigator.'

She covered her mouth, smothering a moan with the handkerchief. 'It won't help.'

Mark stood up and looked down at her. She couldn't be much older than his Jess. He closed his eyes and rode the wave of anger churning in him. 'Why won't it help?'

'Because he used somebody else's name—probably to impress me.' The words were little more than tears.

Mark couldn't see what the big issue was—apart from a cracked heart, which would heal. It was *her* body. If the creep didn't want anything to do with her, she could make the decision on her own. He clenched his fists. 'You liked this guy?'

'Yes,' she breathed. 'I truly did like him. Lots. So much it hurts to think about him.'

Mark sighed. Women always getting attached at the drop of a hat. He wanted to tell her to get on with her life, but the soft light that danced in her eyes for this lover of hers made Mark's gut ache anew for Clare. Why didn't Clare look at *him* like that?

'He probably has some connection with the guy whose name he used—unless it was some movie star.' Mark tried to smile. 'What name was it?'

She raised her eyes to his.

Mark could count his heartbeats. That look riveted him to the spot. He watched her mouth, so like Clare's, form words.

'It was yours.' Fiona took a breath. 'He said he was *Mark King*.'

Mark stood rigid. His lungs ceased to function. He stared at the young woman in front of him and a quake of anger rumbled through him.

'I found out he wasn't you, of course. But now I'm left with nothing. No name. Nothing. I don't know what to do.'

'He used *my* name?' This opportunistic pig had used his name to romance this poor young girl off her feet? Heat suffused Mark's blood. 'Describe the guy for me.'

'Tall, dark and really cute.' Her eyes lit up and she stared past Mark. 'He had this cute birthmark on his butt.'

Mark turned towards the door. That was more than he needed to know. 'Age?'

'He was a bit younger than you.' She looked away. 'Sorry, I didn't mean—'

'No problem.' He shoved his hands into his pockets. 'When did this all happen?'

'Six weeks ago, now. At the local café.' She looked up at him, her eyes full of hope. 'Can you help?'

His fists clenched. He didn't need any more details; he had a fair idea where to head for the culprit. Mark dug his nails into his palms. 'I'll see what I can do.'

Mark's mind churned with the possibilities, and there weren't many. The most likely candidate was someone from his own company—which explained why Clare knew he was after her company. One of his men who was reconnoitring Trans-Inter had slept with her sister.

He clenched his fists. Sloppy. Very sloppy.

King punched the floor-number on the elevator. His blood boiled in his veins. Of all the stupid idiots. He flexed his fingers. What sort of idiot did he have working for him, who would not only use a young woman like that, but tempt fate by compromising the company *and* using *his* name? He gritted his teeth. He'd tear the man to shreds when he got his hands on him. How had he thought he would get away with it?

He stared at the panel where the red numbers advertised the floors he passed. Whatever Clare was up to, she'd had plenty of time to work on it. Six weeks! The whole deal could be compromised. He thumped his fists against his thighs. All because some brainless idiot couldn't control himself. If she'd got some private investors interested in the company, he might find himself empty-handed.

It certainly proved to Mark that he should trust his instincts. He had known from the moment he set eyes on Clare she was after something—probably out to distract him until she'd saved her precious little company from him.

What she didn't know was that he was up to her challenge, fully prepared to go the distance, and more than willing to tackle whatever she had planned...

And her poor sister. If someone had taken *his* sister for a ride like that he'd do anything to get the bastard. Mark's muscles tensed.

The lift doors opened. 'Mrs Thompson. In my office, now.'

'Yes, sir.' She rose tentatively.

He strode to his office and held the door open for the woman. She was still gathering papers from her desk. 'This is urgent, Mrs Thompson.'

The woman dropped everything and hurried in.

Mark slammed the door and stalked around his desk to face his secretary. 'I want you to look up the file on the Trans-International takeover. I want every man who worked on gathering information in my office in fifteen minutes.'

She stared at him, her mouth all but hanging open. 'But, sir, they could be anywhere.'

'Fifteen minutes.'

'Yes, sir.' She walked to the door and gripped the handle, then turned. 'Is there a problem, sir?'

'There'll be blood on the floor, Mrs Thompson. I guarantee you that.'

'Oh, dear. Are you sure? They're such nice young men.'

Mark glared at the woman. 'Now, please.'

He paced the floor while the seconds dragged by. How could Clare waste time toying with him when she had her sister's dilemma hanging over her head? Had she given up? Or was saving her business from him in this elaborate game of hers more important to her than her own sister's problem?

He shook his head. He couldn't work her out.

Mark cracked his knuckles and focused instead on the satisfaction of solving this problem for Clare. How grateful she'd be. How very, very grateful…

The knock was tentative.

'Come in,' he boomed.

Five men entered the room, trailing after each other in single file, lining up in front of his desk as though they were preparing for the firing squad. In Mark's mood, it was apt.

Mark surveyed them. Their hair ranged from Bondi-blond to chestnut to charcoal. One had a moustache, one a beard and one a very hip goatee. But he guessed it wouldn't have taken long to grow it—and seconds to shave one off.

Mark looked them up and down, his anger subsiding, to be replaced by the annoying fact that he should have asked Clare's little sister for more details.

'You.' He pointed at the tall man at the end. 'Is your hair that colour naturally?'

The man shifted the weight on his feet. 'Yes, sir.'

'Go.'

The man hesitated. 'Pardon, sir?'

'Get out!' He glared at the remaining four. He'd have to rely on one of them cracking. There was no way he was going looking for that birthmark.

The one on the right was the tallest, but beanpole-thin, cleanshaven, with auburn hair. The next in the row was the shortest of the group, sporting the goatee, and he looked as if he enjoyed his food, by his generous girth. Next was the bearded man—average height, average weight. The far left man had the moustache, and a physique that belonged in a gymnasium.

Mark rubbed his jaw. Not one he would have picked for Clare's little sister to fall for. He guessed each of them had something going for him, but he personally was at a loss. Maybe he should call Mrs Thompson in?

He paced behind his desk, casting surreptitious looks at the four men left. He noticed the two on the left wore wedding bands, but knew better than to oust them from the room. They could easily have done the deed.

Another knock on the door.

'Come.' He glared at the men in the row, looking each one of them up and down. How could one of his employees have been so outrageously flippant?

His personal assistant walked in. 'What's this about, sir?' John moved across to stand at the end of the line. 'If there's been a problem with the research, then you should be talking to me. I was head of this team.'

'Well, then, John. Maybe you could answer me why Clare Harrison knew that I was interested in her company before I'd even met with her partner?'

Silence.

Mark crossed his arms over his chest. 'No? Then maybe one of these tall dark men would be kind enough to explain why they went against my directive of keeping business business?'

Silence.

'No? Then maybe one of the men in this team of yours knows why Clare Harrison's sister is currently in a state of distress because she can't contact a man that she had an interlude with over six weeks ago?'

Silence.

'No? Then perhaps you could tell me why he chose to use my name instead of his own?'

Silence.

'No?' He assessed each one of the men closely. 'Then I ought to inform one of you that you have a responsibility to the young woman. Not only to apologise to her for your abhorrent behaviour but to help her with the pregnant state she now finds herself in.'

John lurched forward and grabbed the desk, holding himself steady.

Mark swung away from the men and swore under his breath. 'Thank you, men. I think we've found a winner!' Mark turned and watched the departing men. When the last one had tentatively closed the door, Mark turned an icy glare on his personal assistant.

'How could you do this? You're one of my right-hand men. How is this going to look...?'

John stared at him, obviously struggling to find words. 'Sorry, sir. But...it's not...what you think.'

Mark swung his chair out and dropped into it. 'You deliberately went against my orders. You put a very lucrative deal at risk—'

'Sir, I didn't know about your rule of keeping business and pleasure apart then. I met her at the local coffee shop. I had no idea she was a partner's sister.'

He leant heavily on his desk. 'And using my name?'

'I...I have no excuse there. I was so nervous. I wanted to impress her. What better way than using *your* name?'

'Flattery will get you nowhere.'

John sucked in a deep breath. 'It didn't matter anyway. She didn't even recognise your name. She didn't know of you at all, so it was all for nothing. And once I'd said it I couldn't take it back. Not without her thinking I was an idiot.'

'You *are* an idiot.' Mark stood up again and strode to the window. 'There is no way you can account for what you did. Do you have any idea of what state she's in?'

'Pregnant!' He squirmed in his seat. 'With my child.' He leapt up. 'I have to see her. Tell her everything.'

'Tell her you're fired.'

'For what? Falling in love?'

'Love? I find that hard to believe. Why haven't you contacted her?'

John stared at his feet. 'Okay, I don't know that it's love because I haven't had a chance to find out. But I didn't contact her because you gave me that talk about business and pleasure. You told me I'd compromise my job if I didn't adhere to it. But it was too late.' He fiddled with his tie. 'I figured if I waited... It's only another day or two now and I could see her again. The deal will be over and I'll be free to be with her.'

Mark's anger stuck in his throat. It was *his* fault.

He was to blame for Clare's sister's grief, for keeping the young lovers apart. 'You should have come and explained.'

'I tried. You were adamant.' He glared at Mark. '"There are no exceptions",' he mimicked.

Mark turned away. Only one. Clare Harrison. There was no way he was risking the sweet little deal of snapping up Trans-Inter, but the least he could do was make it right for her sister.

'I get the message. But if this deal doesn't happen because of your stupidity I shall be extremely upset.' He stared out of the window. 'I guess you'll need a job if you're looking after a family, but there's no way I can keep you on as my PA. They'll think I've gone soft.' He jabbed a finger towards the outer office. 'We'll transfer you to another section.'

'Thank you, sir. You won't regret this.' John was smiling. He moved restlessly, as though his feet were ready to run for the door.

Mark tried to smile, but couldn't. 'Go on. Get out of here and make that girl smile. And on your way out ask Mrs Thompson to get the papers ready for Frank Bolton to sign first thing in the morning.'

If Clare Harrison was going to obstruct this deal he wasn't going to lie down and take it. There were still a few surprises left in him.

CHAPTER THIRTEEN

CLARE slumped over her desk and rested her head on her arms. She was running out of time. She couldn't believe this was happening. Sure, the last five or six years had felt like a dream—having the company virtually to herself and taking it from something mediocre to an impressive enterprise—but she hadn't expected to wake up from it. Especially not to this nightmare.

She was going to lose her company, her freedom, everything she'd worked for. More than ten years of her life spent here, all to end like this, flailing around for money that no one would give her without her putting up everything she'd worked so hard for.

She bit the inside of her cheek. At least she'd got her mother a house, and she had a place. She rubbed her face, swiping away the sting behind her eyes.

She had to focus on what she did have. She had her family, and she had Mark King.

She stared at the office door. There wasn't anything she could do to save her position, but she'd fight tooth and nail for the employees, for Fiona to keep her job.

She rubbed her right eyebrow and slammed a fist down on the desk. The deep thud and throbbing pain did little to comfort her, did nothing to erase the overwhelming feeling of helplessness.

She paced the floor. Damn it, what could she do? Could she stay and work under someone else? Or would she sell up her share and move on to another challenge? She squirmed. All the people she knew, all her friends…all left behind.

She opened the office door. 'Fiona, could you get me some lunch? A salad roll or—'

Fiona was staring blankly at the front entrance. Her face was pale, her cheeks flushed, her eyes wide.

'Are you all right?' Clare darted towards her. She froze halfway, the hairs on her neck prickling.

Mark King's personal assistant stood in the doorway. He looked slightly ruffled, a little flushed and totally distracted.

Clare let go of the breath she was holding. 'John, what a surprise. What can we do for you?' She moved towards him, her hand outstretched in welcome. What was Mark up to now? Was the limo downstairs, waiting to whisk her away somewhere quiet and romantic?

John held his hands behind his back, but Clare had spotted the bunch of red roses. There was a flutter of butterflies in her chest. She turned back to her sister. 'Fiona—we have a guest.'

Fiona's eyes were still glazed, her expression unreadable. Clare couldn't understand what Fiona was going through with her body, but she should take some more time off if she was going to space out in the office in front of important people.

'John? Your name's John?' Fiona rose from her chair.

Clare stiffened. Fiona would scare the guy away with the way she was behaving. She wanted the flowers and whatever message Mark was sending her. Her body filled with a warmth that caressed her from head to toe.

'Why did you give me another guy's name? I've been looking for you.' She turned to Clare. 'And you *know* him?'

She nodded vaguely, her mind tossing her sister's words around her brain. 'This is Mark King's personal assistant.'

John stepped forward and around Clare, bringing the flowers out from behind his back and holding them in front of him. Fiona rounded her desk and reduced the distance between them, her mood vibrant, her eyes glistening with happiness, her mouth smiling—something Clare hadn't seen for so long.

Realisation hit her and her mouth dropped open. John was the mystery lover!

'I didn't think you cared.' Fiona burst out, letting the tears flow down her cheeks, and she flew into his arms.

John wrapped her in his embrace, breathing her in, dropping the bouquet to hold her close. 'I was waiting for the right moment.'

Clare covered her mouth. Her chest was so full

for her sister she thought she'd burst. She'd never seen anything so sweet and moving in her entire life... Her heart ached for Mark's arms around her.

'Now?' Fiona's voice was a muffled sob of joy. 'Is now the right time?'

'Hell, yes.' John smothered her sister's mouth with kisses. 'I would...have come...the next day... if King...hadn't driven home...his policy.'

'Which policy is that?' Clare couldn't help herself. Any insight into the man might help their relationship—and she was buzzing now from head to toe for him.

John seemed to just notice her. He lifted his head from the crook of Fiona's neck. 'The one where he doesn't mix business and pleasure.'

'I've heard about that one.' Clare looked down at her hands and found herself totally at a loss as to what to say next. 'So this is your...this is him? But how...?'

'It was Mr King.' John planted more kisses on Fiona's forehead, her eyelids, her cheeks, her nose, her mouth.

Clare's buoyancy dropped to her toes. 'King?'

'I don't know how he found out.' John pulled Fiona closer. 'I swear sometimes that man is incredible.'

'I told him earlier,' Fiona bubbled. 'I couldn't help myself. I was crying and he comforted me. It just came out. I must have sounded like a blubbering idiot, but he didn't bat an eyelid. He was so nice…he said he'd help.'

A warm glow spread through Clare's veins at Mark's consideration towards her sister, then she froze. 'You *told* him someone had used his name?' She stared at the ceiling. Her sister had told him they'd thought it was *him*!

'Yes.' Fiona kissed John again, oblivious to the significance of her words.

Clare's body sagged. Now he knew what game they'd been playing—that she'd entered into some stupid ploy to confront him with her sister's predicament. A chill swept over her. He wouldn't want to know her at all!

Her chest ached and she touched her lips. She'd never feel his lips again. They'd had their last kiss.

Clare sauntered into the suave hotel, hanging off her cousin's arm dutifully. It was the worst time for it, but a deal was a deal. If he wanted her to go to some posh party with him to make a statement, then so be it.

'This place is awesome.' Paul's voice seemed deeper. He nodded to the formidable doormen, and they passed unhampered.

Clare stared at her cousin's back as he took her hand and dragged her into the throng of people. Moving around the kitchens of all the finest restaurants, hotels and clubs, Paul had connections everywhere. Which was handy for his nightlife as well as his career.

Clare struggled to pull oxygen into her lungs. She should be poring over figures at home, not be out on the town, but she owed Paul and, as he'd said, the contacts he made here could make his career.

The party was definitely upmarket. The designer clothes screamed wealth, as did the glittering jewellery, the exquisite venue, and the twenty-piece orchestra.

Clare spotted several designs she'd seen in the latest magazines that Fiona had brought home. She darted a quick glance at her simple dress and decided on the spot that she had to buy more clothes.

Paul pulled her close to him. 'Let's find a table.'

She nodded. She was glad she was useful for something. If only she could be as useful to herself and work out some brilliant solution to her money problem. She didn't want to stand idly by and let someone walk off with all her hard work without a fight.

They found a table in the back, where thankfully it was a tad quieter. They ordered drinks and watched the people around them.

'What's up, Clare?' Paul nudged her. 'You seem totally somewhere else.'

She was desperately trying to be. She'd had a couple of drinks to commiserate her failure to buy Frank out before she'd left home, and she was planning on

more. And if she could get her mind off Mark King
at the same time...

Mark had gone out of his way to fix Fiona's problem—for Clare, or for his own peace of mind? She
didn't know what to think any more. Her mind and
body were muddled with facts, with feelings, with
hopes, and she kept coming back to the fact that
he'd caused the mess in the first place!

She wanted to hate King. But she missed him.
His smiling eyes, his voice—him. And every inch
of her craved him. Her lips, her hands, her mind,
her entire body. It wasn't fair. Why couldn't everything be straightforward?

'Sorry.'

'Don't sorry me.' Paul nudged her and smiled.
'Just smile and make out you're some confident so-
cialite.'

Clare laid her hand over Paul's on the table and
leant against his shoulder. 'I'll do my best.'

She didn't know why Paul needed her. Her cousin
would be quite okay-looking if he'd cut his dark hair
occasionally, and his olive skin was fine, if only
he'd shave off the whisper-thin moustache. She
guessed he was trying to look French to accelerate
his career.

She closed her eyes. All she could see was Mark
King. He'd got to her. She could feel him, almost
smell his tangy cologne, almost hear his voice.

'Hello, Clare.' Mark's voice shot through her.

She bolted straight. 'What?' She looked directly

up into deep dark eyes. His mouth was pulled tight, his jaw set, and the white silk shirt he wore had several buttons undone, revealing a light scatter of hair on his oh-so-muscular chest. He had one hand in the pocket of his black trousers; the other had a woman attached.

'Fancy meeting you here!' Sasha's voice pierced the music. Her nose was pointing up and her eyes were definitely looking down at Clare.

'Yes, fancy.' Clare had to look twice. There was no doubt tonight of the girl's intentions. Her backless red dress clung to her every curve and her four-inch heels gave her the extra height to look Mark almost in the chin.

Clare let her eyes wander up to Mark's face.

His brow was creased and his grey eyes were stormy. 'I didn't know you travelled in these circles.'

Clare heard the challenge in his tone. 'I could say the same of you.' Probably trying to impress the young Sasha, showing that he wasn't quite over the hill yet by crashing a yuppie party. She resisted the urge to create more distance between herself and Paul—if Mark was out with Sasha that all but screamed where he was at. And it wasn't with *her*.

She ran her eyes over where Sasha held Mark's arm and her stomach churned. Sasha's long fingers held him firmly, possessively, and he wasn't resisting.

'Business?' she asked.

Mark raised an eyebrow. 'Not quite. You?'

She swallowed hard. There was a chance that she and Fiona hadn't been so far off the mark at the beginning—Mark might well be the womaniser they'd thought him to be. She met his gaze. 'Of course.'

'You know Sasha.' He nodded to the woman beside him, then gave Clare's companion a raking assessment. 'And this is?'

Clare turned towards Paul. 'A friend.'

Paul smiled his most ingratiating smile. 'Who's this?'

'This is Mark King.' She prodded her cousin under the table. If he did something to embarrass her now she'd string him up and give him an earful.

'The fabled Mark King, hey? In the flesh.' Paul rose and took Mark's hand in his and shook it. 'Heard a lot about you.'

'I'd say the same, but—'

'But we have to get going.' Clare stood up. Her hand bumped her glass. A dark stain streaked across the tablecloth. She darted Paul a silent scream.

She didn't want Mark to know she was out with her cousin, for goodness' sakes. Where was her pride? And if King was going to gallivant around the town with a mere girl on his arm, whose purposes were as transparent as glass...

'I have an important meeting in the morning.' Clare poked Paul's shoulder. She stepped out from the table and swung towards the entrance. She found the floor a little uneven as she moved.

'You go, Clare.' Paul patted her shoulder. 'You get some shut-eye. I'll manage here, if you're all right to get home?' Paul darted a look at the crowd of untapped potential contacts.

Clare knew she couldn't ruin the rest of his night on her account. She nodded. 'Sure. I'll grab a taxi.'

Paul pulled her into a hug. 'Thanks,' he whispered.

Mark could take it as he wanted. She bit her lip. Any chance with him would already be ruined. Now Mark knew what game of revenge she'd started on him, for Fiona, he wouldn't want anything to do with her. She turned. 'Nice meeting you again.'

She turned and pushed her way through the crowd—away from Mark, Sasha and Paul. She held her cheeks with her hands, hoping it would help her focus.

She stopped. How could she have let herself get carried away and have that last drink? Of all the times to get tipsy! Her life couldn't get any worse.

She closed her eyes and let the music throb through her. Mark was with Sasha again. If there was nothing between them then why were they out together? She froze. Why did she care? She and Mark couldn't hope to have anything going now, now he knew what she'd done. Even if they did, he wouldn't entertain Clare as a serious relationship. She'd portrayed herself as a woman of seduction, not a long-term partner. Sasha fitted more into his 'proper' lifestyle. She was perfect—for him, his mother and his lifestyle.

She surged into the crowd again, praying for escape.

A hand on her arm pulled her around. 'Whoa. Slow down. What's the hurry?'

Clare stared mutely into Mark's dark eyes.

His voice hardened. 'You seemed to have been taking it easy until I came along.'

Her mind jerked. 'Really?' She met his gaze.

'Yes. It was *very* interesting. What game are you playing with that poor chap?'

'Game?' She almost choked on the word. Was he driving it home? Guilt squirmed in the pit of her belly and heat suffused her cheeks. She raised her chin. The plan had been made with all the right intentions—to right a wrong for Fiona, not something petty and shallow. He had to see that.

He moved closer to her. 'You like games, don't you?'

His words were a warm whisper on her ear. A shiver of awareness careered down her neck and her breasts tingled. 'I don't know what you mean.' She dropped her gaze and stared at her black heels. He deserved something for getting her sister and John together. She took a deep breath. 'I have to tell you, you did a good thing.'

He looked taken aback. 'I did?'

She had to bite the bullet. 'Fiona and John—thank

you.' She squinted, trying to clear her mind. There was something she was missing.

'No problem. So, who was that guy?' He jabbed a thumb back the way she'd come.

The room blurred.

His hands were on her shoulders and his eyes bored into hers. 'Has that guy got you drunk?' A muscle in his jaw twitched and his lips thinned.

She couldn't help but smile. He was jealous! She felt a bubble of warmth rise in her chest. '"That guy" happens to be my cousin.'

He seemed surprised. 'What sort of cousin is he?'

'The really annoying sort.' She leaned into his hold. It felt so good to be supported, and with all the confusion behind them—no more Fiona-baby problems—she was free to give in to the feeling.

'He should know better.' Mark glanced behind him. 'Let me take you home.' She closed her eyes, letting the weariness that had plagued her for days wash over her. Home sounded good. Her warm, snug bed was what she needed.

She swallowed. 'What about Sasha?'

'I'll put her in a taxi.'

'Do you think she'll appreciate that?' Clare could imagine Sasha's attitude at being ditched for her again. 'You could put *me* in a taxi.'

'I think she'll understand. You need a stiff coffee and some fresh air. I don't think a taxi is going to give you that.'

Clare wiped her hair back from her face. 'I don't think she'll be very happy with you.'

He rubbed his hands along her shoulders and back down her arms. 'Why's that?'

'She likes you.' His hands worked their magic along her sensitised skin and Clare couldn't help but watch his lips.

'I know. Do you?'

'Does it matter?' But Clare couldn't help but smile. She touched his very sensuous mouth with her fingers, tracing them, remembering the feeling they evoked.

Mark grabbed her wrist and yanked her fingers back. 'It does to me.' He stared at her lips, his eyes burning, then his lips descended on hers as though the fight he'd been having with himself was lost.

It was a hungry kiss. Mark plundered her mouth with a heat and a passion that was instantly met by her own. She wrapped herself around him, her hands climbing his back and clawing his hair, losing herself in the wanton desperation of her body.

He enfolded Clare in his strong arms, pulling her hard against his body, stifling all thought.

Mark pulled away, leaving her mouth burning with fire, and her heart pounded painfully for more of him, much more of him.

'Wait right here.' Mark stood her against a wall. 'I'll be right back. I just have to tell Sasha what's happening.'

Clare leant against the wall and closed her eyes.

Her lips still burned for Mark and her body ached in places she hadn't thought could ache.

'Come on.' Mark's voice moments later was deep and inviting. 'Let's get out of here.'

CHAPTER FOURTEEN

THE sleek Saab coupé suited Mark King. It was black, smooth, and had a sexy scent all of its own, like he did.

Clare closed her eyes as Mark slipped into the driver's seat. The onslaught of emotion, the inescapable fact of the closed space, the isolation, the privacy, was almost too much to bear. She didn't know whether to be scared of what she felt for him or whether to embrace it.

She wouldn't want to do anything she'd regret later, but the probability was she would—she had a track record that highlighted her miserable luck with men...

A warm hand on her shoulder woke her. She opened her eyes to Mark's dark ones, inches from her own. 'We're here.'

Clare took Mark's offered hand and swung her legs out of his car. She straightened, staring at the concrete poles that stood at large intervals, cars between them, at the ceiling covered in pipes and conduits. 'I thought you said you were taking me home?'

'I have. This is *my* home.' He smiled. 'I'll fix you

a coffee.' He took her hand and led her to the elevator. 'Want something to eat?'

Her stomach groaned its approval. 'What are you offering?'

'I make a mean fettuccini.' He punched the button for the lift and turned to her, his eyes shining.

Clare couldn't think of a man less likely to be found in the kitchen with an apron on than the King of takeovers. 'You cook?'

'Yes, and you don't have to sound so surprised. I can do kitchen as well as boardroom, thank you very much.' The elevator doors opened. 'I'm good at pasta. And pasta. And then there's pasta.'

Clare couldn't help but laugh. 'Pasta will be fine.'

Mark smiled and steered her into the elevator, his palm resting in the small of her back and staying there. He pushed a key into the panel and punched the topmost number. The penthouse. He could easily own the entire building...

Clare shivered. What was she doing? She touched her head. There was something she should be thinking about, but for the life of her she couldn't grasp the elusive thought.

'Problem?'

Clare turned to him. 'Just worried about my virtue.'

He raised his hands in front of him. 'It's all yours. As my mother will tell you—I'm the perfect gentleman.'

'Are you, now? What about in the limo?'

He sobered. 'Clare.' He gathered her close to him. 'I'm not going to ask you for anything you're not prepared to give freely.'

She opened her mouth, then closed it. She hadn't heard that line since high school, and the sincerity behind it warmed her heart. She smiled and brushed her lips against his. 'Thanks.'

The lift doors opened.

They stepped out directly into the apartment. It was big, bold and screamed bachelor. The furniture was modern, black and stark against the white walls and rugs. Clare kicked off her shoes and felt the smooth polished timber floor with her toes.

Mark moved over to the stereo system while Clare glanced around the room. It was so obviously professionally decorated—the lack of anything personal was a dead give-away. She moved past the abstract paintings on the wall to the full-height glass windows that ran the entire length of the open-plan area.

A tune began, slow and melodious—it caressed Clare's body and her muscles relaxed. It was such a contrast to the wild beat of the party.

The view of the city from his window was glorious. The vista was covered in thousands of lights, some no more than pinpricks while others were big and bright. She took a deep breath.

Her skin prickled in anticipation and she knew he was behind her, watching her. Her pulse fired at his body heat, so close to hers, but she continued to stare out of the window at the lights of Melbourne.

'You like it?' Mark's voice was deep, and right behind her. He placed his hands on her bare shoulders.

Her stomach fluttered. 'How could I not?'

'God, you're beautiful.' He swept her hair up and planted his warm lips on her neck.

Her nerves sang at his touch. Clare wanted his hands, his lips, his body on hers, could hardly wait...

She hesitated and bit her lip. She should be establishing the parameters of their relationship, not falling into his arms. 'That sounds like a line, Mr King.'

'I didn't mean it to be.' His lips trailed down her neck and across her shoulder.

Clare took a breath. 'I'm not like every other woman.'

'Tell me about it!' He swung her around. 'I can tell you in all honesty that I've never met a woman like you.'

All thoughts fled her mind as he ran his tongue over his lips. What the hell! She wanted him, fling or not.

Mark pulled her close and wrapped his arms around her.

She slid her hands around his neck, laying her head on his shoulder. It was broad and strongly muscled, made to lean on, to weep on, to rest on—if you were the right woman. She breathed in his cologne, the unique spicy scent that was him, and prayed she was the one...

They moved to the music and his mouth brushed over her hair, and down, pressing firmly against her throat, breathing hot kisses in the hollow where her pulse pounded erratically.

She felt desire stir in him—as it had stirred in him in the limo, as it stirred in her now...a wave of yearning that spread down her stomach, over her tingling breasts, down to her toes.

This was crazy. She'd been hurt enough. She glanced up at his dark eyes, filled with promise, and she knew she couldn't refuse him—the sensual curve of his mouth, the remembered taste of him. Her hands itched to explore him. She couldn't refuse her own needs.

Besides, there was nothing to fear from Mark King. Absolutely nothing at all.

Time melted away for Clare. The music finished and Mark held her gaze with an almost hypnotic intensity, setting off every spark in every nerve, consuming her in desire.

He ran a hand down her arm, over her bare skin, and lifted her hand to his mouth. He kissed her palm, tasting her with his tongue, moving it along the sensitised flesh to her wrist, as though absorbing intimate knowledge of her through the lines on her hands. She shivered.

He met her eyes and lowered her hand, pressing the flat of her palm against his chest to feel the wild beat of his heart. 'Did you want that coffee?' His voice was deep. 'Or the pasta?'

Clare couldn't help but smile. He was offering her a way out of the passion they were evoking. 'I want you,' she whispered, and she stood on tiptoe and took his lips gently, running her hands up his chest, his hot body only a light shirt away.

'Sure?' Mark's lips plied hers with delightful mastery and his hands followed the shape of her curves as though memorising her.

'Yes,' she murmured.

His strong fingers trailed up her back, and then down again, lowering her zipper with them. He stroked the bare skin of her shoulders with his thumbs, pushing the straps across and down until her black dress fell to the floor.

Mark drew a ragged breath, stepping back and allowing his eyes to saunter over her body and the two strips of black lace that covered her. 'Clare...' It was a resonating cry of need.

He traced the line of her cheek with his fingers, drawing her closer, touching his lips to hers gently, almost reverently.

Clare couldn't wait. Her hands impatiently tore his shirt from his trousers, fumbled with the buttons. She wanted to feel his hot, hard body, wanted to hold him, taste him.

She kissed him. Hot, hard. Dispelling control and inviting his passion. She teased his tongue with hers until he was invading her mouth with urgency.

She pushed the shirt from his shoulders and ran her fingernails lightly down his back, touching the hot breadth of his muscles, grazing his tanned skin, wanting to know every inch of the man, the body, needing to reach into him, to truly know him.

She felt his muscles tighten and she pulled away. His compelling dark eyes blazed with a searing hunger, his need resonating through the powerful promise of his touch.

He swept her up into his arms, scooping her off the floor and striding to his large bedroom. She was weightless, lustful, buoyant.

She hesitated. Was she just another notch on his bedhead? Mark nipped her lip with his teeth, sliding her down his hard body until her feet touched the floor and her legs pressed against the satin-covered king-sized bed. Could she risk it?

He slipped away from her, kneeling down before her, kissing her stomach. His tongue travelled along her naked flesh as his hands caressed her thighs, then behind her knees, then moulded her bottom, tugging the lace down. The tenderness of his touch was exquisitely unbearable.

His kisses followed where his hands had been, driving her mad with desire. She wound her fingers in his hair and dragged him upward. He willingly followed, teasing her nipples through the black lace of her bra. Then he claimed her lips again, drinking in her need as he flicked her bra clasp and dropped it to the floor.

Clare rubbed her body against his and delighted in his sharp intake of breath. She ran her hands through his hair and down his back, then skimmed them around his waist. She tugged his belt loose and drew the strip of leather out slowly from his trousers, meeting his eyes.

He watched her with an intensity that charged her.

She trailed her fingers over his chest, playing with his chest hair, his nipples, his navel. His skin rippled into gooseflesh under her touch and she exulted in her power over him.

She worked her hands lower. Her heart leapt at the sound of success—his waist stud popping, the rip of his zipper. She rubbed a leg up his thigh and worked his trousers down with it as she moved until he was completely naked.

'I want you so much,' he whispered.

She responded instantly to the desperate longing in his voice. She brushed herself against him, running her fingers over the cords running up his neck, exulting in the sheer maleness of him, breathing in his cologne, his pure male scent.

He groaned, searing her with his stormy eyes.

Rightly or wrongly, he made her feel incredibly special, and the overwhelming need to return the favour urged her on. She placed her hands on his chest and pushed him backwards.

He collapsed onto the bed, taking her with him. Flesh against flesh.

She took his mouth and plundered it while her

fingers tingled with tenderness as she caressed him, pleasuring him, stroking, softly exploring, revelling in the intimacy. She let her hands tell him how she cared for him, wanting him to know and feel how special he was. It was sexual. It was erotic. It was unbelievable.

'I've never met anyone like you before,' Mark murmured, his voice deep and throaty.

Clare smiled. 'Good.' His muscles rippled under her fingertips. His body was so responsive. She just couldn't stop touching him.

He groaned and rolled her onto her back, smothering her with wild kisses. His hands were seductive, sensually gentle on her, erotically knowing yet unhurried, savouring every part of her, revelling in every quiver as he moved down her body, his lips trailing where his hands had been.

The thrall of being exquisitely aroused was blinding. Clare closed her eyes and let sensation take her where it would.

The sound of her breathing filled her, mingled with his, the spicy scent of his cologne, her perfume and their lust, creating an erotic chorus that sang through her veins.

Her thighs quivered against the hard strength of his and he took her lips again, drinking in her warmth. He moulded her softness to his, slipping between her legs, their bodies entangled.

She held her breath, her emotions wild, a swirl of fierce desire. She locked her arms around him as he moved against her, sending rivulets of heat cascading from her loins to her toes. Need screamed through every nerve, sending sharp bolts of desire streaking through her. She arched her back.

She gasped at the feel of him as he entered her, at the solid strength of him filling her.

Mark reached for more sensation, driving deep, stoking the wild friction of heat, until the beat melted into rolls of sweet chaos.

Clare was floating on waves.

Finally she lay still, anchoring herself, moving her hands through his hair. He pressed his lips against her neck, his breath coming in ragged gasps.

Neither spoke, but the silence was beautiful, full and complete. Mark rolled off her and wrapped her in his arms, pulling the covers over them. He kissed her again on her neck, just below her ear. 'I knew it.'

'What?' she whispered.

'You're one hell of a woman.'

Clare smiled and snuggled into his warmth. She couldn't imagine anything more perfect than lying in Mark King's arms. Life could only get better.

CHAPTER FIFTEEN

THE morning sun shone brilliantly through the windows, illuminating the bedroom and Mark's face, relaxed and soft in sleep. He was so perfect that Clare couldn't resist touching his jaw, kissing the light stubble, his mouth and his ears.

'Morning,' he murmured. 'You can wake me like that any time you like.'

She pushed her hair out of her face and smiled. 'Is that an invitation to stick around?' She couldn't think of anything nicer than spending her nights with Mark.

He smiled at her. 'You're so beautiful.' He stroked her cheek with feather-soft caresses. 'I can't believe you aren't married.'

'Ditto.' The familiar twinge of fear stabbed through her happiness. 'Sometimes people don't turn out to be who they appear to be.' Josh was still a vivid reminder of what lies and heartbreak loving a man could cause.

'You've got to trust someone some time.' He stroked her forehead, running his finger along her right eyebrow. 'Why not let that be me?'

Clare stared into his gorgeous grey eyes. He was right. She'd never loved anyone before; she'd always figured it was too risky. But lying here in bed with Mark, a tide of warmth sweeping over her, she knew if she was to name what she felt for him—she swallowed hard—love would be what she'd call it.

Her heart swelled. Could she finally have fallen in love, with the *right* guy? She touched his lips with hers, brushing them softly, and all the pain of the past melted away, leaving only Mark and her, and love.

She *could* trust him. She felt lighter just thinking about it and snuggled closer to his warm, safe body.

She wished she could stay in bed with him, like this, for ever. But there was a meeting this morning—with the mob trying to take Trans-Inter away from her.

'Talk to me, Clare.'

She knew he was just the person she needed to advise her on how to save her company. *If* he cared. And if he was feeling anything like she was they had something special, maybe even a future.

She took a deep breath. It was now or never. 'You know I've got this company? Well, I don't exactly have it. I run it. But I own a share of it.'

Mark smiled. 'Yes, I know.'

'You might think it's silly, but I've put everything into that place.' She played with the hair on his chest. 'I was ten when my father left us,' she blurted.

'I'm sorry.' Mark stroked her hair.

'We had to go and live with my widowed aunt. Mum couldn't cope financially on her own. Together they struggled.' She took a breath and glanced at Mark. His brow was furrowed.

'What about this?' He traced the scar on her eyebrow with his warm fingers, his eyes soft and deep.

Clare lowered her lashes. 'It's nothing.'

He caught her chin with her hands and tilted it, holding firm until she raised her eyes and met his. 'Really? I find that hard to believe.'

She sighed. 'It was my father.'

She felt him recoil, his hands dropping from her face. She'd never told anyone before. No one. She rolled over, turning her back on him, the ache in her throat threatening to smother her.

'Hey.' Mark held her shoulder and pulled her back to him. 'You want to talk about it?'

She stared at his deep dark eyes and swallowed hard. 'Dad was leaving us,' she rushed. 'He'd met some woman and was leaving us to it.' She touched her scar. 'I stupidly ran after him. He was in a hurry. He pushed me into a door.'

'Hell.' Mark wrapped her tightly in his arms and kissed her on the forehead.

'You don't understand.' Her voice cracked. 'It was my fault. If he'd loved me enough he wouldn't have gone.'

Mark's eyes widened. He pulled her to him and held her. 'Clare, you know that's not true. It wasn't you. He had issues—he had his own life. You can't blame yourself.'

She stayed in his arms for ever, listening to the

beat of his heart and letting the tears fall. He rubbed her back and held her until the tension melted out of her.

'Mum had three jobs,' she finally said, swiping at her damp cheeks. 'As soon as I was old enough I left school. I had to. She was wearing herself out and there was no way I could help her *and* go to university.' She took a deep breath and pulled back. 'I fell into a great job with this man called Frank Bolton. I started as a gofer and worked my way up.'

Mark stroked her shoulder with his thumb, sending tingles anew running down her spine.

'He put me through night school and promoted me to Personal Assistant. I could support Mum and Fiona.' She ran a hand down his taut belly, feeling more relaxed than she ever had. 'When Frank got a divorce from his wife I used some money that was left to me and bought out her lesser share. The company was in bad shape then.

'Frank stepped back and I took over. I was twenty-four-seven on the job and I took it places.' She paused and stared him in the eyes. 'I love that company. I'd do anything…'

Mark expelled a breath. 'So you're going to finally come clean over what game you've been playing…?'

'Game?' Clare echoed, staggered.

'You can cut the act.' His voice was gentle. 'We both know I'm buying your business out from under you today. But what I don't get is why seduce me this last week?'

Clare swallowed.

Her brain balked.

He couldn't be.

She had to have heard wrong.

She stared at King and her blood chilled. The man who had seen Frank was Mark Johns—the third party who was out to rob her of her future. Mark *and* John. Her stomach turned.

The planes on his face blurred. *He was the enemy!*

King, John, Fiona. Her mind jerked. Of course! King had been preying on her company from the start. Why the hell hadn't she thought about how those two had met? Why John had been hanging around at her end of town?

Coincidence? Not a chance. She'd bet her life on it. She was such a fool. If only she'd seen the truth sooner...

She swung herself off King's bed and swiped the moisture from her eyes. 'Oh, I wouldn't want to spoil the ''game'' for you. It's for you to find out.' She snatched her underwear off the floor.

Her clothes were everywhere. Visions of what she'd shared with King over and again last night haunted her. She tried to keep her hands steady as she dressed, concentrating on breathing, slow and deep, until she was clad.

King propped himself up on his elbow. 'I've

driven myself mad with guessing. I can't work you out.'

She managed a smile. 'Tough.' She strode through to the lounge and picked up her dress, cringing. Why didn't she ever learn?

'Is this some female thing?' He was close.

Clare spun around.

King leant on the doorframe, every naked inch of him reminding her of what they'd shared. Her body roused at the memories and she gritted her teeth against its response, the overwhelming urge to enjoy him again.

King radiated a relaxed sort of arrogance that chafed, leaving Clare with the harsh fact that he'd known all the time. Every kiss, every touch had been assessed as her 'game'—she didn't even know what that meant any more. She stabbed her feet into her high heels.

She shrugged. She couldn't trust herself to speak. Her throat ached at the irony—she'd managed to do it again. Fall for the wrong man. And, boy, had she picked a doozy this time! Mark King had to be the worst man to fall in love with on the planet!

'Look, can't we talk about this?' His tone softened. 'Openly and honestly? After last night, I thought—'

Clare shot him a look of contempt. The last thing she wanted him to bring up was last night!

He cleared his throat. 'It's obvious you're upset—'

'Give the man a prize!'

He stepped forward. 'Whatever it is, I'm sorry.'

Clare stabbed the elevator console and spun to face him. She clenched her fists at her sides. 'Sorry? Let me tell you, King. We're way, *way* past sorry!'

'I don't understand—'

The doors opened and Clare stalked into the lift. 'Don't worry. You will. But it will be too late!'

The doors closed on King's face. No matter what, she wasn't going to let anyone walk off with her company. Least of all Mark King.

CHAPTER SIXTEEN

MARK felt the doors close like a punch in the gut. He shook his head, trying to shake off the distinct feeling he'd missed something very important.

He straightened. It was probably another chapter in Clare's game, designed to perplex him, muddle his mind and put him off his form. The idea clawed at him. He'd thought the games were over. He'd thought they had something, a special something, that might have become so much more. Obviously Clare didn't feel the same.

He balled his fists against his thighs. If she thought that he was about to have a problem keeping business and pleasure separated because they'd spent an intense night together, she had a surprise coming. Business always came first.

He stared at the elevator doors. Had Clare had a breakthrough in how she was going to keep him from her company? Did it have anything to do with their night together? Was it *all* part of her plan?

Mark closed his eyes. He might have been carried away by the moment, by her, by her intoxicatingly gorgeous lips, her deep blue eyes and the wicked way her hands had touched his body, but he had known that they were safely in *his* apartment—not *hers.* Any sort of recording device or blackmail were off the list—he wouldn't mind airing their lovemaking. God, she was something else...

He squeezed his eyes shut, straining for a hint of what brand of game she was playing, his blood rising at the sheer powerlessness of not knowing. It was a feeling he was unaccustomed to and didn't like.

Mark knew without a doubt getting pregnant wasn't her game. Aside from her sister's predicament, it wasn't her style—and it wouldn't save her company. By the time she could confirm it the company would be signed, sealed and sold.

Trans-International was the perfect company for him to command and conquer, and there was no way he was going to give it up because Clare Harrison was a stubborn fighter with an agenda and the most distracting smile. Trans-Inter was a deal close enough to home to ensure his name stayed on everyone's lips.

He pressed his fingers against his temples. She was an enigma. Why the hell had she revealed her past to him like she had? That hadn't been any game, any act—or else he'd slept with an Oscar-winning actress last night!

Clare's sobs had ripped through him, tearing at him, driving home how helpless he was against protecting her from her past. His chest tightened. When she'd cried in his arms it had been all he could do to stay in control. If he ever got his hands on her father...

Mark picked up his shirt off the floor. He rubbed his stubble, staring at the lift doors again. She'd acted surprised when he'd told her about today's takeover, as though she didn't know what was going on.

He strode into the bathroom. It didn't make sense. Clare *knew* he was after her business. She knew because a man had used his name to seduce her sister. He stared at his reflection in the mirror. They'd known it wasn't him who had done it.

His heart slammed into his chest.

Clare's efforts to get him to go home with her... Fiona coming into the bedroom... Clare disappearing... God, they'd thought *he'd* slept with Fiona! He clenched his fists.

He stared at his wide-eyed reflection. The truth was staring right at him—*Clare hadn't ever known anything about him and the takeover!*

He grimaced. This wasn't going to change things. He *never* mixed business with pleasure. The takeover was business as usual. Clare would understand that. *He* understood that.

He took two deep breaths and punched the idiot in the mirror. She'd been pouring out her life story to him so *he* would help her out of this mess!

Mark turned away from the jagged image, the burning pain in his hand almost as bad as that in his chest. He clamped his other hand over his bleeding knuckles, fighting off the burden. She was just another woman, anyway. A bit much to handle at times, but still like the rest.

Mark held his hand under the water and blood ran in the sink. Then there was Sasha. Nice, quiet, proper Sasha. She'd make the perfect little wife for him. She'd be there with his slippers and his dinner ready, even if the cook had made it. His mother loved her. Jess loved her.

It was time he settled down. He wrapped a towel around his hand tightly, finding satisfaction in the pressure, in the pain, in the action itself.

Clare wasn't going to make a difference to his plans. He snatched up his shaver and glared icily at the mirror. She knew more than anyone that business was business.

Clare stalked into the foyer of Trans-Inter acutely aware that she had only two hours to save it from the biggest exterminator in the business. King would take every part of her business and rip it to shreds, then sell every piece off like some scrap-dealer.

She faltered at the front desk, the weight of her heart in her chest making breathing difficult. Only a couple of hours until she saw the lying, conniving jerk again.

Tanya looked up. 'Good morning, Clare. Fiona rang and said she wouldn't be in.'

Clare clenched her teeth. Just when she needed her. She could imagine her sister, wrapped in her lover's arms, smiling, happy, content. She shook herself. She didn't need anybody. She never had and never would. She coughed away the dry ache in the back of her throat.

Fiona had John now. And her own life.

'And Paul left a cryptic message,' Tanya added. 'He said, "Thanks for the intro. Sasha's the best."'

She swallowed hard, stifling the irony that even her silly cousin could fall in love, while she was a walking disaster.

Clare straightened. Damn them all. She didn't need it. 'Tanya, get Frank on the line and get him in here early. And get my broker.'

'Right away.' Tanya smiled. 'Problem?'

The word hit her in the chest. King's irritatingly handsome face jumped to her mind. 'No.' She spun on her heel and stalked into her office.

This had to work.

She covered her mouth with her hand, as though the action would smother her stupidity. She'd fallen for the guy—lock, stock and flaming barrel—and now he was turning the gun on her, on what she held most dear.

She'd been an idiot to run off at the mouth like that last night. She'd told him way too much. She shook her head and bit her lip. And she'd been about to ask *him* for help to save her company! She tried to laugh, but the sound caught in her throat, bringing tears to her eyes.

How could he have used her like that?

She and Fiona had been right from the start. She should have quit while she was ahead, while she was still emotionally intact. Mark King was a womanising creep in the first degree. It had taken a little longer for him to show his true colours than they'd expected—if only she'd seen them earlier she wouldn't have put her damned heart on the line again.

She threw her chair back, the castors skating it backward against the wall. That was it, then. No more men. No more relationships. She was useless at them. She'd get a cat and call it quits.

Clare slumped into the chair. It was time to accept she was not cut out for a family life. One disaster after another had proved that, and this one topped the lot.

She rubbed her eyes, struggling to thwart the wave of self-pity threatening to break. She could blame it on alcohol, but she hadn't had enough to lose herself. In some ways she wished she had, then she'd have passed out rather than making mad passionate love with him all night.

'Frank's here,' Tanya's voice chimed.

Clare stared at the intercom. She took a deep breath. 'Send him in.' She crossed her fingers and looked skyward. *Please let this work.*

The door opened and she rose, plastering a smile on her face. She wanted Frank to feel totally at ease with her and the plan she was about to throw at him.

She wasn't going to lose her company to King, even if she'd already lost her heart.

CHAPTER SEVENTEEN

THE room was a cubicle of vacant space usually used by the staff for their parties. But there wouldn't be any laughter today. Far from it.

Clare sat at the far end of a rectangular table they'd moved in especially for the most important meeting of her life. Her back was to the wall, the chair the enemy was to sit in directly across from her.

Frank sat next to her, his hand over hers. They watched the minutes creep by on the clock on the wall, saying nothing, both knowing the significance of the meeting.

Finally, Tanya opened the door. 'Come in, gentlemen. The owners are waiting for you in here.'

Clare pulled her hand from Frank's and stood up, knowing only too well the importance of a first impression. There was no way she was going to have anyone think she wasn't up to this, especially King. She held her breath.

The door swung wide and several suited men walked in. Each gave her a cursory glance, as though she was inconsequential, which from their perspective she was. They moved to the chairs around the table, King trailing behind the pack.

King's grey suit stood out amongst the darker ones, as did his tall, muscular shape, his dark hair, his deviously handsome face and his piercing eyes.

He stood at the head of the table. 'Miss Harrison. I wonder if we could talk before we start negotiations?'

'No, thank you. I'm fine.' She sat down, staring at the documents in front of her, the print blurring.

'We may be able to make a deal here.'

Clare gave him a cool glare. 'I would rather sit on a tigersnake, Mr King.'

The suited men had the decorum to cover their surprise with a multitude of coughs. They sat down as King sat, perfectly choreographed, as though they'd practised the move. Clare figured they might have, knowing King and his exactness.

Clare could feel his eyes on her.

The suits shuffled papers and one man stood up. 'We're here today for Mr King, to negotiate the purchase of Mr Frank Bolton's share of Trans-International.'

Clare fixed what she hoped was an icy glare on King. His hair was brushed back, every strand in place, his calculating eyes were bright and his suit irritatingly immaculate. And the arrogant jerk was unabashed by meeting her eye to eye.

A shiver coursed down her spine.

'Mr Frank Bolton.' The suit gave Frank a defining look. 'Have you got the documentation?'

'Yes.' Frank stood up. His ears were reddened,

his nose flushed. His eyes lowered and his hands were unsteady as he slid the papers across the table to the suits.

King lunged forward, stretched out a hand and intercepted them.

Clare held her breath.

He flicked through the papers, his brow furrowed. 'This isn't right. Where are the rest?' King raised his eyes slowly.

Frank turned to Clare. His eyes were wide and his eyebrows furrowed—he was obviously tossing the ball into her court.

Clare stood up. 'Well, it seems, Mr King, you made one assumption too many. In your conversation with Frank when you made your offer, you omitted to qualify how much of Frank's share you wanted.'

He stared at her, his eyes strangely empty of emotion. 'You've bought enough to be majority owner.' King's voice was strong and formal.

'And to be in control.'

King swung towards Frank. 'I thought you wanted to retire?'

'I do.' Frank cleared his throat. 'Clare has offered to buy a number of my remaining shares each year, *if* you don't want to negotiate the purchase of them.' He stared his hands, held tightly together on top of the table.

Clare stood abruptly. 'So I guess you won't want

Frank's share now?' She gathered up the papers in front of her. 'The door's there. Feel free to use it.'

'On the contrary…' King smiled dangerously.

Shivers of desire coursed involuntarily through her, accosting her with memories of last night and the delights she'd experienced at his hands, his lips and his body.

Clare scrutinised King. Her mind buzzed. What could he do with Frank's remaining shares? He wouldn't be able to slice and sell if he didn't have control! She hadn't considered him still buying them. She figured he'd storm out thwarted and she'd never see him again. She sank back into her seat.

She stared numbly at the suits, shuffling papers and passing pens, as first Frank and then King signed the contracts. Blood pounded in her ears and her mind raced in circles, trying to grapple with the significance of this unlikely turn of events.

'So that's it.' King clapped his hands together. 'If everyone would leave the room, I think Miss Harrison and I should talk tactics.'

Clare stared after the suits leaving, her confidence sinking to the tips of her toes. Frank gave her a backward glance, offering only a shrug.

The door closed and she spun to face King— whatever he had planned, she wasn't going to fall for it this time. 'What are you doing?'

'Having our first business meeting.'

'Our what?' The room suddenly seemed too

small. 'You're not having anything to do with this company, or me.'

'On the contrary. I have a stake in this business and, like it or not, sweetheart, I'm your partner.'

She opened her mouth. She couldn't imagine anything worse than being stuck with King and his annoyingly perfect body. 'But you'll be busy with all your other interests. You won't have time.'

'Actually, I'm thinking of appointing a board of executives to manage my empire, so I can concentrate on where I'm needed most.'

'Here?' Her voice broke and she bit her lip to stifle her body's response to him.

'Yes. Right here by your side. Could you show me my new office?'

How could she see him every day? Her body was reacting to him already. *And* he was hostile, *and* the enemy. And despite everything she knew it wouldn't take long before she weakened again and found herself in his arms.

'Of course,' she said with an air of calm. It was a game, surely. He couldn't be truly interested in sticking around in Frank's office after his stately one in that high-rise. Putting up with the shonky airconditioner in summer, the wicked gas bills in winter, and all the struggles associated with battling for a dollar.

Clare sauntered to Frank's old office, acutely aware of King's eyes on her. She paused at the door and took a deep calming breath, fighting down the onslaught of insults she wanted to throw at him for his callous treatment of her. She turned with a flourish. 'Here it is,' she bit out.

He smiled at her, letting his eyes drift over her.

She shifted her weight. She hadn't dressed for seduction, she'd dressed for battle, and if he was still turned on by her, tough. That was his problem. She couldn't care less that his grey suit was impeccably tailored on his gorgeous body, or how smooth his freshly shaven face looked, or how tempting his lips were.

Clare's body reacted, and her mind reacted, taunting her with images of him naked. Frissons of heat spiralled through her body and it was all she could do to remain calm and composed. *She didn't care what he looked like naked. She didn't care what he made her body feel.*

King sauntered into the office, moved around the tired oak desk and sat in Frank's high-backed leather chair. 'The room has definite potential.' King nodded and surveyed the room. 'A bit of paint, pull out a wall...'

Clare opened her mouth.

'Tell me, Clare. If you had a choice, what would it be—owning your own company or a chance at love?'

She snapped her mouth shut and glared at him, a lump in her chest. 'I don't believe in love,' she finally said, her throat aching. 'And how dare *you* talk about love? As if you know what it is. You go about tearing people's livelihoods away and selling them off. You use people when it suits you and toss them aside when it doesn't.'

King dropped his gaze, a glimmer of pain in his eyes. 'I take it that's your answer?'

'Damn right it is.' Clare's eyes stung with the intensity of her feelings. She stared at her shoes, counting her heartbeats, willing the tears away—she did not want to show weakness in front of King, of all people.

She heard the rustle of paper, a pen scrawling, and then King pushed a paper across the desk. She glanced up. 'What's this?'

'This is your company, Clare.' King rose from the chair and strode to the door, his mouth set in a grim line, his eyes cold and hard. 'It's what you want. Be happy.'

Clare stared at the paper. He'd transferred Frank's shares to her! Her mind buzzed with the sheer magnitude of it—the company was *all* hers.

Clare's mind darted to expanding markets, purchasing more vehicles, more employees, more branches... And it sounded empty. Hollow.

She faltered. Because she hadn't earned it? Or because Mark had given her a priceless gift, her dream, without provocation, without reason? She stared at the doorway. It was what she'd always wanted and he'd known, *and cared*.

She hesitated. She closed her eyes and tears pricked. Could she open herself to hurt again, let pain accost her life again? But then, she wasn't going to hide, wasn't going to give up on life or on love.

Clare yanked open the door and burst into the hallway. She spun left and right, but Mark King was gone.

CHAPTER EIGHTEEN

'SECURITY? Clare Harrison. You have a man coming down dressed in a very expensive grey suit, answering to the name of King. Detain him, will you?'

Clare smiled and put down the receiver. She straightened her trousers and flicked the top button of her blouse open with shaking fingers. Let him sweat for a few minutes, like she was.

She ran her hands through her hair and strode down the hall with all the confidence she could muster. It was time to take a chance.

Mark had his hands on his hips, his harsh tone drifting towards her as she approached. 'You have no right to detain me. I've done nothing wrong. I insist—'

The security guard caught her wave and nodded. Mark turned. 'What's this about, Clare? I'm a busy man.' But his tone was noticeably softer.

'Thank you, Tom.' She waved the guard off with a smile. She turned to King and met his deep grey eyes. 'I wanted to say thank you.' She held the paper up. There was so much power in her hands, so much control. 'But, no, thank you.' She ripped the paper in half and let it flutter to the ground.

The corners of Mark's mouth twitched. 'It's what you wanted.'

She shook her head. 'No. I didn't know what I wanted. I know now.' She moved towards him until she was close, until she could feel his warm breath against her face. She held his cheeks in her hands. 'You.' She brushed his lips with hers and the instant reaction in her body swamped the rest of her speech she'd rehearsed.

It was a kiss for a tired soul to melt into, to drown in. She gasped for breath. 'I don't need a company,' she finally managed. 'I need a partner. And you're the only one for me.'

Mark swept her into his arms, holding her in his strong embrace. 'God, I love you, Clare Harrison.'

She smiled softly up into his gorgeous grey eyes. 'What about kids?'

'What about them?' King kissed her neck. 'You're not going to tell me your biological clock is ticking?'

'No, I was going to tell you yours is.'

His laugh rumbled through her. 'I'm ready, willing and able. But what about you? Can you manage all this and kids too?' He waved a hand around him, then settled it on the curve of her hip.

'Can you?' She smiled mischievously. She could see Mark looking after a brood of little Kings. 'I can manage anything you throw my way.'

'Even my mother?'

Clare's smile faded. She'd forgotten all about her, and that young Sasha. 'What about Sasha?'

'Who?' Mark smiled and hugged her. 'And you can start again with mother. She's not as bad as they make out.'

'They said that about you.'

'And?'

'And they were wrong. You're very, very bad. But I love you anyway.'

He took her hand, stroking her bare fingers. 'What's the story with you and rings—or lack of them?'

Clare stared at the floor. 'I guess they signify commitment in a relationship. I've never had that.'

Mark dived into his suit pocket. 'Would you consider committing to me?' He flipped the top on a red velvet case, revealing the most dazzling diamond ring Clare had ever seen.

If she let herself, she could so easily be offended that he'd second-guessed her. 'You knew!'

'No,' he said softly. 'I hoped.' Mark wrapped her in his warm safe arms and kissed her until the past no longer mattered.

'So will you marry me?'

Clare pouted. 'I don't know. Is this a hostile take-over?'

'Come home with me and I'll show you exactly what you'll be committing yourself to.'

Clare smiled. She couldn't wait. And she couldn't wait to discover what else was in store for them. But, no matter what, she knew they'd have each other.

BETTY NEELS

Harlequin Romance® is proud to present this delightful story by Betty Neels. This wonderful novel is the climax of a unique career that saw Betty Neels become an international bestselling author, loved by millions of readers around the world.

A GOOD WIFE

(#3758)

Ivo van Doelen knew what he wanted—he simply needed to allow Serena Lightfoot time to come to the same conclusion. Now all he had to do was persuade Serena to accept his convenient proposal of marriage without her realizing he was already in love with her!

Don't miss this wonderful novel— brought to you by Harlequin Romance®!

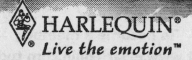

HARLEQUIN®
Live the emotion™

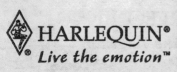

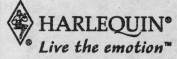